SING,
NIGHTINGALE

SING,
NIGHTINGALE

MARIE HÉLÈNE POITRAS
TRANSLATED BY RHONDA MULLINS

COACH HOUSE BOOKS, TORONTO

Originally published in French by Les Éditions Alto as *La Désidérata* by Marie Hélène Poitras
Copyright © Marie Hélène Poitras and Les Éditions Alto, 2021
English translation © Rhonda Mullins, 2022

First English-language edition.

Coach House Books acknowledges the financial support of the Government of Canada. We are also grateful for generous assistance for our publishing program from the Canada Council for the Arts and the Ontario Arts Council. Coach House Books also acknowledges the support of the Government of Canada through the Canada Book Fund.

LIBRARY AND ARCHIVES CANADA CATALOGUING IN PUBLICATION

Title: Sing, nightingale / Marie-Hélène Poitras, translated by Rhonda Mullins.
Other titles: Désidérata. English
Names: Poitras, Marie Hélène, author. | Mullins, Rhonda, translator.
Description: Translation of: La désidérata.
Identifiers: Canadiana (print) 2022024989X | Canadiana (ebook) 2022024992X | ISBN 9781552454480 (softcover) | ISBN 9781770567351 (EPUB) | ISBN 9781770567368 (PDF)
Classification: LCC PS8581.O245 D4713 2023 | DDC C843/.6—dc23

Sing, Nightingale is available as an ebook: ISBN 978 1 77056 735 1 (EPUB), 978 1 77056 736 8 (PDF)

Purchase of the print version of this book entitles you to a free digital copy. To claim your ebook of this title, please email sales@chbooks.com with proof of purchase. (Coach House Books reserves the right to terminate the free digital download offer at any time.)

For my mother
For my father

'This dull, blind land. And all the blood, the milk, the chunks of crusty afterbirth.'

— Anne Hébert, *Kamouraska*

I

BY THE CLEAR FOUNTAIN

Under the clouds, the village of Noirax looks like a little theatre. Cardboard sets, a stage on which to deliver lines, and puppets awaiting a hand to bring them to life, send them scurrying right to left, then left to right, until they disappear into the wings.

A distant melody can be heard, carried on a woman's voice. A joyous refrain that in no way foreshadows the brutality of the last verse, which will fall like a guillotine's blade.

The surrounding forest is made of words, with secrets buried in the spaces between them and entwined around the roots.

Curtain.

hick smoke rises from the estate's ancient chimney, blending into the gathering clouds. Along the forest path, the warm body of a hare by the neck in one hand, a rusted trap that has seen better days in the other, the father walks onto the set.

Spring is early this year; the buds are sprouting over the dead leaves that a mild winter never managed to dislodge. In the forest, one walks on a carpet of ancient moss that marks the eras – the Era of the Horn, the Era of the Wing, the Era of the Sheep, and the Era of the Hoof – and that can be read like growth rings on a sectioned trunk. Summer is returning like a promise kept, never betrayed. The three jennies of the estate, heavy with foal, will give birth in a few days. There will be visits from the young cep merchant and the renderer. The tender thorns of the blackthorn tree will be macerated to make the Troussepinette that will be drunk until September. Camellia flowers will bloom. There's the fountain and its pond scum to clean out, down to the bend in the marble goddess's hip. There's the sycamore hedge to propagate and train so that the knotty branches keep climbing toward *He who observes us from on high, his sights trained on us until our last moment, never relaxing his watch.*

Let spring come and let the young donkeys bray.

At the manor, there sits on the massive acacia-wood table a plate made of kaolin, local treasure and pride of the village, a precious mineral, fragments of which are embedded in the tombstones and the clock at city hall. Since the kaolin reserves were exhausted, small artisans have settled for producing eau de vie and other regional spirits. On the plate, a gracious hand has placed four prunes, some currants and quinces, and a half-peeled lemon. A bottle of red that is still a little young is decanted in the carafe. There are fresh almonds in their soft hulls, a donkey chorizo in a rustic piece of pottery, and that morning's homemade bread, still soft. A partridge laid out on the checked tablecloth and a sharp knife complete the table. The father sets down the hare against the bird's wing, feather and fur as one, and turns toward the hearth where logs are crackling. There is no need to feed the fire. Before gutting his prey, he rubs his cheek along their downy bellies.

The sky brightens, and an oblique light shines on the father as if through the rose window of a cathedral, striking the metal of the knife. It might be better to hang the partridge to eat later, but already the warm blood is spurting on the flat of his palm.

❧

In his sleep, the father thinks he can hear a jenny bray. He gets up and crosses the wooded area that leads to the enclosure, using a lantern to light his way. As he goes, he chases off young hares with white thighs and cotton tails. The donkeys are immobile in the dawn. He has often hauled on the legs of their birthing foals in the middle of extraordinary nights. They don't turn their short necks toward him, but the father is sure that he has been summoned. He won't go into the forest to mourn Pampelune; he has locked up her memory in the Perfume House, to which he hasn't had the key for many seasons, the births of many foals, at least seven winters and two mayors. Despite the loneliness that weighs on him, he avoids walking past Pampelune's headstone and goes back to the estate without straying from the path on which he spotted the tracks of a sow. The father draws the curtains on the dawn and goes back to sleep in his bedroom.

Late in the morning, a young voice comes in through the half-opened shutter on his window and rouses him from sleep.

À la claire fontaine	*As I walked*
M'en allant promener	*By the clear fountain*
J'ai trouvé l'eau si belle	*I found the water so lovely*
Que je m'y suis baignée	*I decided to bathe*

It's her, the merchant of truffles, amanitas, and chanterelles, who hikes up her skirts to keep him company, her bosom even heavier than it was last spring. *I've loved you so long, I will never forget you.* He joins her in singing and invites her in. The father plans to stuff the chilled partridge with the ceps to feed her. Would she rather he heat some braised rabbit with quince on the coals? While she hungrily devours the rabbit stew, the father is overcome by a desire to feed her berries that will burst in her mouth, to watch their juices run down the flesh of her lips.

After the meal, he takes the merchant to the lake and watches her slip into the pristine water. She is plump, pink, and fatty like ham hocks. She is his son's age or a little younger, with thick ankles and mischievous eyes.

When she emerges from the lake, milk runs from her breasts. To drink her milk, feast on her cherry, press her up against the cold stone of the wall and grow stiff inside her. At her request, drain his seed in the dead leaves. The cep merchant would make a good wet nurse, the father thinks. If he ever has a grandson, he will hire her and once again open the doors to the house where the memory of his late wife is locked away, to let new life drive it out.

Fortified by the merchant's visit, the father puts on his best clothes to go strut through the village. He slips into the blue-grey velvet jacket that brings out his eyes and assembles the rest of the outfit around it: his tall boots in caramel leather, a fedora, and his father's cufflinks. He would have liked to have hitched a horse, but the harnesses in storage are dry and cracked, and all he has left in his possession is donkeys. He is afraid he will get his boots dirty in the mud if he walks. The father thinks of taking the balloon, then reconsiders; he will go to the village by car.

When he leaves the Malmaison estate, it folds down like a cardboard set that has been dismantled.

In the father's absence, the hares stop leaping over the black-thorn roots, the milk curdles, perfumes go off, the bread hardens, the magpies fall silent, the dust settles, and the partridge opens its eyes again. Time stops, dissolves. In the forest, on the shady hillside of Pampelune's grave, frost covers the stones, while in the front, under the sun, primroses, daffodils, and soon the bells of lilies of the valley will climb through the dead leaves, then stop growing as soon as the father's foot steps off the estate.

Halfway to the village, immobile and useless, the Jorle Mill. 'They should get it going again or demolish it once and for all,' the father thinks as he walks by.

☙

It's market day. Rita sells her Jésuite pastries from a red van, Odette washes the leaves of cow cabbage, removes the slugs, and cracks the snails between her fingers, while her husband stokes the fire to make a massive tart. Vendors are already selling Troussepinette and other decoctions, swearing that in their garden, on the sunny side, the thorns from the bushes are as tender as asparagus shoots.

The father stops at the inn for a drop of cognac. The innkeeper offers him pickled herring and a few slices of blood sausage. It is not yet noon, but in the half-light of the bar it is perpetually midnight, and a second glass can be knocked back should the spirit move the drinker. When the father emerges, looking stooped, with his salty breath, he spots an accordionist in the gazebo with trunk-like columns covered in ivy. He is playing a tune that makes sorrow swell in the father's heart. The smell of warm apple and the memory of the milk from the cep merchant's breasts running over his tongue comfort him for a moment. Heading to the post office, he meets the renderer and asks him to stop by to pull a wolf tooth from one of his jennies.

'And I want to castrate the jack.'

'I will come this week then. Sheep to bleed? Heifers to inseminate, bulls to dehorn?'

'No, all I have left is donkeys.'

The coyotes wiped out what was left of the flock of sheep, and the last heifer kept the father fed through the winter.

Three letters are waiting for him at the post office. One is from his son. He is returning from the high country, the Hauts-Pays, after a love story gone wrong. In addition to having his eye colour, Jeanty has his bad luck in love. The father is comforted that he will return to Malmaison, preferring not to imagine him suffering, his heart heavy. He will have to check the stores in the cellar of the estate; they will drink some good bottles together, with game and roasted chestnuts. Jeanty left so long ago … It will be wonderful to see him again.

The second letter annoys him. He will reread it with his monocle, because it goes on forever, in addition to being written in poor-quality ink that has run into the margins. It comes from the back country, the Arrière-Pays, from the hands of people who are demanding a share of his estate, a mention in his will. People have often tried to siphon off part of his fortune. People think he is richer than he is; generally, that suits him, but not always. He knows how to spot the bumpkins and the riff-raff. He will examine the letter in detail and put a notary on the case if necessary.

The envelope of the third letter is stamped with an A in red wax and is addressed with a woman's fine hand. She is offering her services to owners of the surrounding estates: breeder of live-stock (horses, goats, rams, pigeons, and turtledoves), originator of new crops (fungi, vines, aromatic herbs, and ivy). She has been told that the father Berthoumieux, who has just three donkeys left, not even any livestock, may be interested. One year to start a stud farm, a bit less for vines. Trained from a young age on an experimental farm. Breaking, training, and coupling if desired. References upon request. Arriving soon in the Centre region.

A black-and-white photo slips from the envelope. A young woman in overalls rakes a field, holding the rake in her bare arms, which are thin and muscular. There is something so immodest in her eyes that the father has to look away. The handwriting is lively and full of energy, entirely deliberate. And she signs a name that commands respect: Aliénor.

One last drink at the inn. His blue eyes are shining, like a sky on the verge of rain. The accordion player has made way for a bagpipe player. He is wearing knee socks and a kilt, his shoulder-length hair cut in a broom bob. The minstrel's face doesn't inspire the father's confidence. After buying a bag of ripe peppers for the ratatouille, he leaves the village by way of the Jorle and returns to Noirax at nightfall. The set is restored, the water flows in the fountain, and the wind caresses the camellia flowers with the intent gentleness of a hand on a breast. The headlights before him, as the car climbs the hill toward his houses, the father watches the frightened hares take off hither and thither, then comes across a fawn and is moved by it.

❦

By hand, he rolls a few logs at the back of the fireplace over the ashes. He rereads the letters with a magnifying glass to detect every level of meaning and implication, unearthing the traps set behind the hints and the less subtle turns of phrase. The waiting begins: soon he will have company. He will need to hire help to scour the Perfume House while he clears branches, pebbles, and slag outside to house the breeder whose name he hardly dares say, even to himself. He will take her and Jeanty to the village one evening for a dance. Let them get drunk and bond while he feigns interest in the still that produces alcohol on the Grand Place. He will watch the drops fall one at a time, a smile on his lips, recall the smell of the raw spirit from the first distillation of fruit. Then, when he comes back, he will take pleasure in seeing them arm in arm, their cheeks flushed in the noise and the clamour. The lovebirds can settle in the Perfume House, and the cep merchant will be asked to be the wet nurse: that's the plan. It's been a while since the father has given himself over to blissful reverie. Hope springs; it feels good. It makes him want to tug the burgeoning buds, like the merchant's nipples, for spring to be sprung.

❦

In the early morning, the father spots at the end of the road a man who is advancing at a good clip, arms full of tools: the renderer. He left his truck at the bottom of the hill to avoid sinking into the mud. 'So, the wolf tooth?' he says to the father by way of greeting, brandishing pliers. In the field, a surprise awaits them: a foal as fluffy as a teddy bear, born at dawn, is standing unsteadily on its four limbs. Tiny, endearing. A second foal is stretched out on the ground. The father looks beyond the Malmaison estate, focuses on the detail of a far-off valley to wash away the vision of the dead foal, lingers on the neighbouring estate with the budding vines growing on the sunny side of the hill. The grapes are the size of pearls. The renderer's visit couldn't be better timed. If a soothsayer had been there, he could have read the animal's entrails and warned the father. He would have announced that someone was heading to Malmaison to sow chaos. That the bad memories would be replaced with others, even worse. That this young person was already walking toward Noirax, that she was slithering like a garter snake and that she had the power to awaken sap in the old trunks. She is getting closer, agitated, fervent; one would do well to beware. Yes, that is how the soothsayer would have spoken today over the steaming innards of the foal, had his path not led him to the west, to Ouestan, where he was dozing, drunk, on a beggar's bench.

They carry the warm little body to the forest's edge to bury it in a deep hole where tomorrow wild garlic will appear.

The renderer removes the unwanted tooth without too much trouble, but the two men have a hard time castrating the stubborn jack, who hurls himself at the father's chest before biting the other man on the shoulder. When the sterilized blades strike each other, you can hear him bray as far as Finistax. Every time the renderer comes, it ends in a blood bath; the father grows weak at the sight of the gelatinous liquid. He takes a flask from his pocket, and the two men take a swig from it as they watch the animal rear up and flee into its enclosure.

'That donkey is pigheaded,' the renderer says, examining his throbbing shoulder.

'It's just a poor donkey,' the father replies.

He pours alcohol from the flask over the man's wound before pouring more in his mouth.

The father makes chit-chat as he holds the renderer's head as if he were preparing to slit his throat.

The renderer immediately wants to remove himself from the father's presence.

'You will have to forgive me. I have an entire sty of pigs to slaughter two villages away. It will be a long, back-breaking day.'

Getting up, he slips in the blood. He should spread a bit of lime on the stain, but he is eager to leave the barn. The air is heavy at the Malmaison estate. What is not said is much worse than the prudish words that brush the lips.

itting upright, weak from seasickness and therefore fed a diet of salted rusks, Jeanty is coming home from the Hauts-Pays. The nausea began as he was watching the waves, mesmerized by the foaming of the sea, the unfathomable colour he loves, shot through with flashes of ochre. In this blue, carried on a wave, he saw emerge the face of the woman who ran him off. Her profile was revealed to him as if in a cameo of foam, chignon tied, neck straight, lace collar, lobe pierced by a pearl. She had that slippery look of her bad days, an expression he was never able to read. Jeanty wanted to plunge his hand into the rolling waves to grab her locket, then plunge his whole body, while he was at it, until he disappeared into the unctuous blue. How deep is it below the bilge? How far between the floor of the hold and the floor of the sea? Staring into the furious waves, constantly renewed, he leans over the railing, as if hypnotized. Thinking he is going to throw himself overboard, a woman cries out. Two men grab him, each by a shoulder. 'Your time has not come yet, sir. Your services are not needed up there. Here there is bread, wine, flesh, and sweets.' The two soldiers smile with more kindness than the woman he left behind had ever shown him.

After this moment of distraction, he is placed in a cabin at the bow with a bag of croutons meant for the seabirds. Another forty-eight hours before he can set foot on land. Meanwhile, he thinks about walking through the forest to his mother Pampelune's grave, of the logs burning in the hearth, and the local game cooked by his father. Jeanty always returns to Noirax, stays until he suffocates. For him, Malmaison is both a haven and a trap.

Aboard a train as black as her hair, Aliénor is travelling at the same time toward Malmaison. She has left behind the cracked earth of Saud and is now reaching the lands of the Centre. Had she been aboard the ship, Aliénor would have been its figurehead. Tied to the front like an offering to appease the gods, it's their wrath that she would awaken.

Stomach queasy and still looking unsteady, Jeanty finally sets foot on the soil where he came into the world. He has only one suitcase with him. People stretch their arms toward the travellers. He notices the feminine wrists waving handkerchiefs, rosy-cheeked cherubs watching for the return of fathers. The scent of roasted chestnuts and cigars, clean oilskin, and perfumed women: the scent of return.

The two artillerymen who grabbed him hold out a pamphlet: 'If you are still interested in life … ' They wish him good luck for whatever is next, say goodbye, and leave with a purposeful stride to reunite with their boys with snotty noses, little girls stuffed into velvet dresses, exhausted wives.

'They know where they are going,' Jeanty thinks. For him, it's not so clear. His stride always takes him in the wrong direction. Unless Malmaison is where he should put down roots? He doesn't know anymore. His home makes him anxious; he feels like a stranger in the very place he was born. The locket swallowed by the waves comes back to him.

Suddenly, above the clamour, the voice of the man who sired him.

℮℩

The two men are the same height and of similar build. They shake hands, embrace.

'My son, you have become a man,' the father says, moved.

He has that assurance, a booming voice. The moustache and the frock coat add a touch of distinction. He holds himself upright, chest broad.

The same blue eyes, the same loneliness: the physical resemblance is striking.

'Drink, it will perk you up,' the father says, holding out the gourd, a pig's bladder.

The delicacy of the nectar surprises Jeanty.

'Oh! It's not Troussepinette!'

'Fig eau de vie, your mother's favourite.'

The two men get in the car. The father tells him the latest news: upcoming municipal elections, an early spring, flooding, stems flowering. The birth of a foal and the castrated jack. A large plate of almonds in their tender hulls on the table, 'the way you like them. The hearth will have to be cleaned out. Take your time settling in; I have wonderful plans for us.' He wants to see his bloodline carry on and his lineage grow.

After crossing the bridge, through the trees that still have somewhat understated foliage, Jeanty catches a glimpse of Malmaison, separated by a low wall of limewashed stone, looming at the end of the road. Two centuries old, the chimney is smoking, a sign of the life within. Ivy climbs to the gables perched on the roof, shutters pulled back, windows open a crack, a mass of new leaves reaching out from the old shoots made brown by the smoke from the hearth. The roof does not have the opulence of those of the homes in the neighbouring region, a few leagues from the estate. Here they bet on milder weather, made temperate by the forest cover, and they prefer curved tiles in a brick red that faded with the frosts and the drizzle of the century that has passed, to blend in better with its surroundings; the colour of the roof has settled between pink and brown, on fawn. Heavy walls in grey stone, almost ramparts, lightly crumbling at the northwest corner. Past the gate, the gravel road stretches into a clay road by which Jeanty and the father come and go.

The lush forest reveals itself as the backdrop and seems almost impenetrable. The day is dying and, in the beam of the car's headlights, hares bolt, so they drive carefully. A large bird of prey passes overhead, spreading its wings. Glides for a moment before swooping down on the abundant small game.

Where does the buzzard go when the curtain falls?

&

At Malmaison, at the centre of the load-bearing wall, there is an immense painting by Poedras. The artwork and reality now converge, one the miniature of the other, down to the mood of the sky, except for the ivy growing backwards. The artist did not orient the ivy toward the light, which is not a lapse in taste or an error in realism, but rather the artist's signature.

While the father goes down into the cellar to find a bottle of a local Armagnac with the distinctive taste of the terroir, Jeanty steps toward the towering canvas by the local artist, keeper of the memory of Noirax. While the painter's works adorn many walls in the home, this canvas is the first one visitors notice. It cannot help but be seen, and it is as if, as soon as you enter Malmaison, you are invited to enter a second time. Almost all the villagers have a painting by the current Poedras, or one painted by his father or his father before him. The talent for drawing came down through the blood: the Poedrases are artists, father to son.

The painting of Malmaison spent a long time turned toward the cold stone wall in the attic. It was thought to be a failure, because of the inaccurate orientation of the ivy, until it was noted that many of the artist's paintings had this anomaly, the plants turning away from the sun, and by extension men from divine light. *He who observes us from on high, his sights trained on us* has never held sway with the old painters, indifferent as they are to all forms of mercy, in particular the sort bought with a prayer.

After toasting their reunion, the two men start downing their drinks in long swigs, increasingly exaggerating their length.

'The woman from the Hauts-Pays,' the father begins. 'She has an evil eye. And a leaden heart. You did well to leave her.'

'She was the one who threw me out.'

'We'll find you a new one. Trust me. For now, let's drink. Tomorrow we will go boar hunting.'

The donkey has been kicking in rage for two days. In the distance, they can hear him braying. His sheath and inner legs have grown red with all the bucking. Blood has flowed down to his pasterns and coagulated in a thin crust.

At the end of the meal, to accompany the cheese course of Tomme and Comté, they open a bottle of vintage Monbazillac with an exceptionally sweet nose. The golden wine flows over their tongues and loosens them. The father sees that Jeanty closes his eyes to better taste it, and that his manners have become more refined during his time with the woman with the evil eye. As their cheeks grow rosier, the conversation comes alive. The father confides that he dreams of becoming mayor of Noirax. To serve and control, order people to better propagate the vines, oversee the production of artisanal wines.

'These shameless people in their raggedy underthings trying to sell you the worst plonk as if it were a charming local vintage,' he laments. 'It is far too early to distill the thorns from the black-thorn, everyone knows that; the shoots are not tender enough yet, and the Troussepinette they make from them is so bitter it prac-tically stings your eyes. The buffoons and the clowns with the booth at the market are raking it in. It has to stop. Just like the busker who plays the bagpipes so badly he makes the innkeeper's wine go off! That bum should be replaced by that pretty vielle player, and there should be legislation to ensure it. One needs to have earned one's place on the stage and know how to do honour to it. You don't just waltz through the door ... And why not a puppet theatre while we're at it! I was born in Noirax, I've given this land a son, my wife's body feeds the forest floor; I have an instinct for what this village needs, because I am bound up in its history. I know the secrets of its soil. There is no more kaolin in the reserves, but the artisanal know-how remains. Let's import it and process it here, with the expertise we have. It will give the villagers work, and they will stop pretending to be winemakers. They will be proud again. The truth, my son, is that I have grown bored in this forest, among the colonies of rabbits, the ghost of your mother, and the view of the mill that lies still in the distance. Spring may be here, but I found winter endless. Life needs to return to Malmaison, I made that wish, and here you are. In my arms, my son!'

Their closeness rekindled by the Monbazillac and the alcohol that went before it turns the conversation from politics to matters of the heart. There are so many flowers, donkeys, and deer here on the Malmaison estate, but not the shadow of a gentle woman to caress their flanks. All that remains is the eternal memory of the wife and the smell of her perfumes shut away in the adjacent building to which the key has been lost. A lady's gaze needs to rest once again on the primroses, her delicate nose burying itself in the bell of the lily of the valley. A woman's body dipping into and emerging from the lake. Otherwise, this entire setting, which exists through the father and continues through the son, all the magnificence of this place, is a total loss. They need a woman in a white dress to walk along the trail, to return wreathed in the dawn's light, the hem of her skirt damp from the dew. The path is trodden by only one man, who leaves to go hunting and comes back with warm baby hares, their pulse fading under his thumb.

Hunting or contemplating Pampelune's grave. Strolling along the road to find food or to honour the dead. That weighs on a person. There are many more things to find in the forest: fruit, dreams, secrets. What is needed is the cries of as-yet-unborn children to scare the partridges so they leap into the hand to be killed. Let nature grow wild and new characters enter the scene.

'Why don't you tell me now why you were driven out of your home?' the father asks. 'A well-off, well-born, handsome young man in good health is hard to find ... what happened?'

In the tall, narrow house along the canal, typical of homes of the Hauts-Pays, where they lived with his mother-in-law, Jeanty reports that they often closed the shutters, but no child came. After some time, the mother-in-law stuck her nose in. One evening, when her son-in-law came home from the pub, she announced that he should turn around and leave by boat that very night. It was cold in the house; dampness wept from the old stones. Jeanty's bag was packed. His wife was crying upstairs, her tears rolling into a pretty, embroidered handkerchief while the wretched mother, at the bottom of the stairs, was already stomping her feet, misery in a starched dress, eyes hard as stones, a dried prune where her heart should be.

'Damn those shrews! Now build up your strength, my son. Tomorrow, we hunt.'

Jeanty spun the story to go over better, but it was anything but the truth. One afternoon when the wife had gone to her embroidery club and the mother-in-law was at her cards club, he did not go to the pub to watch the rugby finals as he had said he would. Coming home earlier than planned, the mother-in-law had discovered him nonchalantly rummaging through her powders and tints, dressed in the scullery maid's clothes, his crimson lips humming an octave higher than usual.

The story is different, but the ending is unchanged: the couple's union was broken, and Jeanty was chased off.

Glass after glass after glass, anecdote after secret, they drink until they collapse from fatigue, until their eager blue irises turn to liquid.

ে৩

First light. They both slept badly, Jeanty still dreaming of the waves, nauseated and melancholy, the father engrossed in the fresh memory of the visit from the young merchant with full lips opening to announce the price of chanterelles and to sing.

Je voudrais que la rose fût encore au rosier
Et moi et ma maîtresse dans les mêmes amitiés

I wish the rose were still on the bush
And my sweetheart and I were still in love

When they reach the heart of the forest, they come upon a cluster of morels, set down their bows, and take a moment to breathe in their mild, earthy, mushroomy scent. There are so many mushrooms on the estate that the game they hunt is infused with their taste, along with the taste of the herbs that grow there: thyme, sage, marjoram. Jeanty sections the stems with a knife, presses his nail into the thick leaves, and breathes in his fingers to conjure the smell of Pampelune.

He hasn't shot an arrow in a long time; the bow initially seems awkward in the young man's hand. While warming up, he pinches the skin on his arm and burns himself on the snap of the cord, but the arrow plants itself in a tree trunk, a sign that he hasn't completely lost his touch.

Berthoumieux father and son head further into the forest, branches whipping their temples. A litter of coypu squeal at the lake's edge, making the father grimace. This pest is spreading on the estate and is impossible to contain.

He practises hunting by tracking, ideal for the lone wanderer who knows the woods like his mother's face. One generally needs to be armed with patience to engage in this style of hunting, which involves waiting until the animal passes rather than circling its territory and forcing it to flee along a trail under watch. At the

Malmaison estate, the boar roam in a nourishing paradise. Careful not to disrupt the cycle of mating and reproduction, the father will take one or two per season, selecting by sight the non-dominant males, those that have fresh wounds from a fight lost to the alpha. Spurned as suitors, condemned to wander alone, they are no longer of use to their kind, and some of them end up on the father's table.

The success of tracking depends on the subtlety of the hunter. No sudden movements, constant vigilance; you need to forget you are there for the animal to appear. One day, a lead sow, busy spreading her secretions on the ferns and the trunks, making the land stream with them and scenting it with her elixir, came to sniff the tip of the father's boots as if he were a rock, so close that at one point he rested his palm on the animal's withers and then buried his hand in her bristles. Her coat was the colour of Pampelune's hair. She was the one who sooner or later would trigger the heat among the herd's other females. She left as soon as the father removed his hand from her hide.

Father and son are hidden behind a row of shrubs that line the wallow, a puddle of muddy earth where the piglets loll like children in a chocolate fountain. Not far away, there are signs that some have upturned the earth in search of bulbs, acorns, and tubers, chewing on slugs.

The father hands Jeanty the binoculars, still without a sound. Like sentries on duty, they have been nearly immobile for an hour. Then the son spots an animal roaming on the other side of the wallow. He prepares his bow, pulls back the string, closes one eye.

'Not the sow, Jeanty!' the father warns. 'Can't you see that she has no whetters or cutters? That's what the binoculars are for. Look over at nine o'clock instead to the fat boar nosing around a root, probably devouring some carrion. Go on, pierce its heart! Hit it under the shoulder.'

The arrow whistles; the animal collapses on its side, at the base of an ash. The pride of a father, the astonishment of a son.

'We will make head cheese and blood sausage; we will braise the jowls. Better still: we will cook the head!'

Keeping his father fed, Jeanty is somewhat reinvigorated. Hunting is the nature of things. He wants to learn to take care of the manor, help his father with upkeep. He kneels, places his hand on the animal's warm body and smooths its fur, ready to tear the thick fur, to slit the hide to quarter the animal and carve it up. Before planting the knife in the bristles, he asks:

'Shall we skin the beast, father?'

Now is the time for hands to get dirty; the heart can go back to sleep.

∽

Wearing a black dress and a maid's cap and apron, another woman, one of no particular age, arrives at the Malmaison estate: the harridan. She sits for a moment at the fountain's edge and contemplates the Perfume House. Once the door has been opened, we will discover that the plaster on the walls inside has flaked. That animals that came in through the hearth are roaming, moaning, and copulating. That the story of this house cannot be written solely in the past tense. It is in the present that tales come to life. She has often secretly wished that fire would carry off the Perfume House, with all the memories it holds, and the mould as well no doubt, until the frame collapses. She is haunted by an uneasy feeling: there will be movement here, sudden arrivals, animal and human lives colliding, accidents, a great deal of agitation, disorder, and noise.

The harridan uncrosses her legs and stretches out at the feet of the marble goddess who watches over the fountain. The woman's figure has filled out over the past few years; that is what happens when desire abandons you. The morning sun has gently warmed the light ivory of the fountain, and she can feel its benevolent heat down to her slip, which she has hiked up to mid-calf. She turns her face for a moment toward the sky of Noirax and closes her eyes. Herbs grow in the cracks of the marble, humble camomile flowers with yellow buds that she rolls between the thumb and index finger of her right hand. The goddess of the fountain tips her pitcher, and the water joins with that of the basin in an endless cascade.

In Noirax, siblingship is organized around the wet nurse's milk. They avoid marrying those who, as children, drank from the same source. At Sunday dinner, the wet nurse is seated to the right of the child she is feeding. The harridan nursed so many young lips with her breast. Jeanty suckled on them until the age of eight, sometimes hiding from Pampelune, until he grew ashamed. She has made almost all of the villagers milk brothers and sisters. In times of famine, she even fed an entire family, right down to the grandpa. The woman has healed minor wounds, scrapes, and wasp stings with her milk. And when the source ran dry, and kinship through milk was no longer, the wet nurse became a housekeeper.

❧

When she runs her hand through the cloudy water of the fountain, algae clings to her joints. Frozen in this incline – neck outstretched, ankle exposed, her hand sweeping the water – she is recreating the gestures and pose of the marble goddess. Under the stone streaked with thin veins resides the memory of a woman who lived on the estate under another reign, among other livestock, in the arms of another father Berthoumieux. The one who once offered her grace to the sculptor so he could capture her for eternity is Héléna, the first desiderata, a silent servant with olive skin, kaolin cheeks, and almost violet hair, with whom the father of the father fell madly in love.

In the Era of the Sheep, this father got it in his head to honour her beauty by having a fountain built at the vanishing point of all perspectives, so that his eye could caress the goddess's inclined neck whenever he looked out the window.

He sent for a sculptor from Île Rose, reputed for its marble, who spent a protracted year with his model. In the shed where the father stored the traps, hung his prey, and tanned animal hides, Héléna draped herself in a veil and stretched out on the sturdy table without ever speaking a word. Her abundant hair was topped with a laurel crown braided by the matron in an effort to transform her into the daughter of Dionysus pouring her jug into the basin. The sculptor also fell under the charms of Héléna, who suddenly found herself at the crossroads of the two men's desire. The father's instinct for domination awoke his hunting and predatory drives.

To make the object of his desire his alone, he pursued her relentlessly through the forest of Noirax. Was it a game, was it mating season, a transgression, an affront? A new land to conquer and possess, for as long as the sting of desire lasts? At the end of the hunt, the young woman collapsed in the red needles, clutched at the ferns, the roots, whatever her hand could find. Sap and semen ran together under the full moon. Strange how the mud smells good. Spreading its wild scent of liquid sun and green frog, the smell of spring held in the soil. The mind must be kept busy when one is dragged into the mire, a small window in the head open for a brief escape. Or one can sing to forget what is happening. If one can't speak, it requires a lot of concentration to hear the melody in one's head, or to count *the shining stars and astral bodies, offering the cloudless night their procession in the heavens.*

Dieu qui leur donna la vie et l'éclat,
Dieu qui leur fixa la course et le pas
Sait aussi quel est leur nombre
Et ne les oublie pas.

God who gave them their life and brilliance
God who gave them their course and their pace
Who knows their number
And who does not forget them

Like a cat playing with a half-dead mouse, the father took her into his arms every night, after each new death. A rag doll, wax doll, straw doll, a bride worn out from the violence of a traumatic wedding night, feet limp like those of a doe felled by a hunter's bullet, then felled again, hunted again, collapsing again, reviving and dying every night.

Afterward, she had to find the strength to get back up and go see the sculptor in the shed so he could care for her scraped elbows and knees.

Héléna, the first desiderata, has not been forgotten. Nor have any of the others who followed.

Upon seeing her belly growing rounder, the matron barred Héléna from Malmaison. She would have to be hidden somewhere. The father cleared out the second building on the estate, a small unoccupied manor that would become the Perfume House, so that Héléna could move in until she gave birth. A child was born and was taken into the woods to be set on a nest of humus – cradle or grave, no one knew.

Soon after, the fountain, the pride of the father, was unveiled to the villagers during a late summer banquet lit by will-o'-the-wisps and the August stars. After having paid the sculptor, the father sent him back to his island, by boat, as one would ship a package to a faraway cousin. He barely had time to admire his work. Héléna stepped toward the fountain, and, contemplating it, placed her hand on her hip, then revealed her neck from under the thick hair fragrant with laurel. Inflamed by desire, the father devoured her with his eyes. She was a shining beauty that the sculpted marble goddess, in all its magnificence, could never capture.

After a fruitful hunt during which the hunting horn sounded eleven times, boars were grilled on a spit. Grand crus and other vintage bottles were opened. The champagne flowed freely; no one drank Troussepinette that night. There was the burning velvet of Armagnac at the end of the evening to satisfy throats. While everyone ate and drank, filling their bellies to bursting, Héléna walked toward the fountain, entranced. She found the water so beautiful that she dipped her foot in. In the Mer Basse, aboard a boat that was slipping through the night toward Île Rose, the sculptor dipped his foot in the water at the same moment, then let himself sink into it completely.

In the early morning, Héléna was found lying in the water of the basin, as beautiful as the night before, as dead as she was silent, drowned in the most sumptuous of tombs.

Il y a longtemps que je t'aime, jamais je ne t'oublierai. I've loved you so long, I will never forget you.

II

SING, NIGHTINGALE, SING

hrough the rolling landscape, Aliénor travels by train, crossing through the land of purple-blue shutters and orange roofs. The land of opulent houses barricaded against the wind near the seaside. A small bastide in stone, a chateau in the distance. The green oxidized copper roof of a cathedral, its towering spires piercing the horizon. Names of bad wines, words with *ek, er, or, ac,* and soon with *ax.* Ruins and brambles, the burnt-out frame of a barn.

In the evening, Aliénor does not pull down the berth to sleep; she advances toward the locomotive to watch the coal burn. Contemplating the black turning to red then to grey soothes her. She throws oppressive memories into the fire, casts off anything that could slow her advance. She has made this trip only once before, going to blossom like a flower transplanted to inhospitable ground. A rerooting in strangely familiar soil is taking place. Soon a flower will bloom with flaming petals.

She still has to switch trains a few more times before arriving in Noirax. Aliénor has all the time in the world and enough dresses to last a few days. She can't wait to feel the cool air of the Centre sting her cheek and lash her legs. Breeder, gatherer, sower of trouble. Animal and plant life springs from her hands. Two nice squat fillies were born in Saud a few days before her departure, so perfect that it gives her pangs in the heart. Hooves made to crush pebbles, a head to weather any storm. A shoulder to help in the fields, if necessary, an abundant mane for a bow, a spinning wheel, the lute. 'Next year, I will go break little Pottoks,' Aliénor thinks, as the locomotive cuts through the dark night, swallowing up coal and spitting out smoke.

Passe, passe, passera	*Pass, pass, you shall pass*
La dernière, la dernière	*The last, the last*
Passe, passe, passera	*Pass, pass, you shall pass*
La dernière y restera	*The last shall not pass*

She never understood why some people abhor the idea of eating their mount, swallowing the heart of their horse with a river of stout. The heart contains so much fury and iron will. Chewing its fibres causes its qualities to settle inside you. Becoming one with the animal in the hereafter, taking in its nourishment to love it until the bitter end: for her this is a natural act. She devoured the once powerful breast of her mare, braised, with gingerbread with mustard spread on it, beer, and onions, the ultimate tribute. She absorbed the protein to allow her to do something big: board this train and travel to Noirax to confirm a terrible rumour that had lit a fire in her breast.

෫෮

Spotting two men coming back along the forest road, bows on their shoulders, frock coats stained red, clutching a boar by the head, the harridan sees that the father is talkative, carried along by one of his good days, and Jeanty has become a young man. Blood mixes with milk in her thoughts, fills the basin of the fountain with pink water, and causes her premonition to resurface again: evil will descend on the young one, and nothing can protect him from it.

Jeanty and his father set up outdoors in the wind and place the carcass on the table where Héléna once lay. To clean the animal, first the hair must be scraped away. The housekeeper brings them a pot of boiling water that she pours over the head while father and son scrape and pull fur in small tufts. They spend a good hour at it, eat a hunk of bread, dried sausage, and a slice of Tomme cheese, then go back to the head to finish it with a small blowtorch screwed on to a bottle of propane. Under the flame, the bare flesh grows taut and takes on a copper hue that already makes it more appetizing. Now they have to trim the interior, debone it, and set aside the brain to make a nice and creamy sauce. They saw off the animal's tusks, cut out its tongue, scald and scrape it too, and everything is ready to brine. The first step is complete.

'It's a shame there is no dog in the manor,' Jeanty says with regret, as he severs a neck bone.

'Give the bones to the housekeeper for her stock,' the father offers as a solution. 'And follow me. I have something to show you.'

The harridan sees them go, their hands stained and their eyes blue. When will she get a chance to be alone with Jeanty to warn him?

❧

The father told his son about his plans to reopen the Perfume House.

'I hired a young lady to take care of the sycamores and the plants, to garden around the estate, and I would like her to stay in the second house if it is still inhabitable.'

The door to the Perfume House is not locked, but it is stuck. Jeanty tries in vain to force it open with his shoulder.

'You are going to dislocate your shoulder, Jeanty!' the father cries. 'Let's go fetch the ram instead.'

'I could swear that, in this life on the estate, time is pickled in the same brine as the boar's tongue,' the harridan thinks when she spots them. Emerging from the shed, armed with a ram like the medieval warriors they are not, they take a run up and slam it into the door over and over. The head is that of a woolly ram that impregnated an impressive number of females in the Era of the Sheep, a time of ewes and lambing, in the age of the goddess of the fountain. The ram's head was attached to the end of a tree trunk for luck. Finally, the door gives way under the impact of repeated blows, and a puff of dust emerges that makes the father spit.

'No one should walk through that door,' the harridan murmurs to herself.

'We should send in a canary as a scout, like in the mines,' Jeanty suggests.

'No,' says the housekeeper, with an authority that surprises the two men. 'It would go to die in the hearth.'

The harridan has been having more premonitions since her return to the manor, set mainly around the Perfume House. She heard the sound of rustling wings and guessed the rest. As soon as the bird is released into the Perfume House, it will look for a way out. When its wing brushes the old lace curtain, the curtain will disintegrate like marble turned to powder, the same for the serge tablecloth. The thin, clawed foot will set itself down and the crocheted fabric will fall apart. The window is so dirty that the bird will not go tap its beak on it in the hopes of exiting that way. It will lose its bearings in the manor filled with memories. The canary will be so alarmed that its confused flight will take it to the back of the hearth. Ash is ash, it does not turn into anything else;

the bird will quietly curl up in it, as in the bottom of a nest of grated pumice. Resigned, its chirping will grow fainter, until it is nothing more than a tiny bell, its only company the ghosts in the portraits. Then it will see, high up, an opening, an aperture that will allow it to extricate itself once it has regained its strength. Hope, and then its little heart and its wings will stop beating. A yellow spot collapsed in the ash like the sun in the sky of Noirax, death as sudden as a kiss. As sovereign as desire.

'Yes, good idea, Jeanty. Tomorrow we will send a canary into the house,' the father decides.

After breaking down the door, the father and Jeanty retrace their steps, leaving the memories in the Perfume House to go stale like old tea. In the bedroom, the window of which opens onto the humid breath of the woods, hanging on the wall, a framed sketch from the last century depicts a man and a woman perched on their horses, one dappled, the other chestnut. The woman, in her long skirt, is riding sidesaddle, both legs resting on the left flank of the horse, which she drives with a German bridle and reins, a firmer hand compensating for the imbalance created by the position of her lower body. Resting on her left palm is the set of four reins, which she holds dexterously, without crossing them. In her right hand is an engraved flask, which she brings to the horseman's mouth to force him to drink in a casual gesture he has not consented to. The expression of surprise on the face of the man who sits atop the dappled horse reveals a loss of control: he didn't imagine being forced to drink a mouthful of eau de vie this early in the morning. Nothing is known of the tie that binds them, but the desire for greater proximity can be seen in how dangerously close their horses are, in the woman's risky gesture, and in the man's abdication. Were they spotted? Who are they to one another? Frolicking widow and widower? First cousins twice over? Milk brother and sister? Well born, from the Noirax bourgeoisie, the woman is in her early forties, the man a few years younger. They are wearing beautiful, sophisticated hats, a boater for her and a bowler for him. She is making him drink because he is riding badly, so he will relax his grip a little. They seem to be alone, at least they are acting as if they are. But the chestnut horse the woman is riding, whose beautiful head is centred in the drawing, is looking at the person sketching the portrait, while the other seems too frightened, no doubt because he is being reined in too tight. Mouth open, teeth protruding, something is upsetting him: the inexperienced hand of the man who is drinking and who will relax as he loses control. It is only the first chapter of their story, but already one can anticipate that he will fall and that the fall will be spectacular. His horse glares at the artist from the corner of its eye. It is not the leading hand that is unwelcome, but rather the person who is observing them to draw them. How was the artist who decorated the Perfume House able to capture this off-kilter moment if the horses were fleeing him and the people merely flitted past his pencil?

It is because they did not pose for him and their passage was fleeting that the artist was able to draw them with sincerity. In short, the sketch has little to do with the original two riders. The artist reinvented their story, brushed up against their truth in revealing his own.

❦

In the middle of the night, the father wakes up in a panic and starts talking to himself: 'We didn't cut the ears flush after singeing the skin! Or add the tongue to the mould! We need to buy eggs in the village for the salpicon. Pork rinds, lard, goose fat! And cheesecloth to wrap the head before tying it and sending it off to be cooked.'

When Jeanty wakes up, he opens the curtains and sees his father, his back to him, his hands rooting around in the boar's head. Outside, on the table where he is working, the harridan has set a knife and two basins, one filled with steaming water and the other with cold water. A few steps away, the door to the second manor is still open. A little beyond that, there is the edge of the forest, its mouth open in an O to swallow them all. Hares hop around the grounds, hide in the roots, pop out of a thicket, take their chances between his feet.

In a different time, the father and the harridan were lovers. At the edge of the fountain, her hair just brushing the water in the basin. The warm marble under her lower back, thighs parted, throat exposed. Never as beautiful as the goddess, but it was spring, winter had been gruelling, and desire had started flowing along with the sap in the sycamores at the entrance to the estate. The father often bet on the horses at a time when the Berthoumieuxs' fortune seemed limitless. He lost almost every time, which made him want a roll in the hay, a game at which he had much better luck. With the harridan, the layers came off down to the skin, even though the air was cool and there was still a bit of snow in the centre of the forest. It happened many times that spring, then the short season of their love came to an end. It was almost another lifetime, and the father barely remembered it, didn't even recognize her. The harridan had changed a great deal.

As he opens the window, Jeanty hears the young donkey bray. Last night at dusk, his former wet nurse visited him, looking worried about bad days ahead. 'She has aged,' he thinks. 'Her face has changed, and her waist has grown thicker.' But you don't forget the one who fed you. Now she wears a bonnet and hides her abundant bosom under an apron, a bosom previously within easy reach of hungry mouths and libertine hands. She flattens it under a bib, creating a thick torso with no discernable shape or contours. Jeanty noticed, amid the furrows chiselled in her features, a worry line cutting across the horizontal plane of her forehead.

'I've come to warn you, my boy. Don't step over the threshold of the house of memories. Pampelune's perfume turned long ago, you can be sure of it. Your memory will give out and bang up against the ceramic tile. You will find no comfort in that house. Someone is coming. She will be the cause of your downfall. Misfortune, dishonour, and worse still. Do not touch her, do not approach her. Do not feed her, and do not let her animals walk your land or grow fat from your pastures. Do not let her cultures invade your world, her shrubs take root in your soil. She is a little bastard with no morals.'

'My wet nurse is mad; she has lost her mind,' Jeanty thinks.

He asks, pleading, 'Are you sure there isn't one little drop in your breast for my lips and my thirst, nothing at all?'

She calls him a boor and a rude young man.

He clicks his tongue; she slaps him feebly. Then pulls out a nipple to comfort him.

❧

Jeanty goes to join his father, who is focused on the task at hand.

'Father, what are you doing so early in the morning with your hands in the head?'

'I was cutting the ears of the boar so that we can heat them with a chaudfroid sauce when we serve it,' he says, turning to his son, a knife in one hand, an ear in the other. 'I want you to go to the village to buy a veal trotter, shelled pistachios, sheep's tongue for the stuffing, bread crumbs, cognac, and eggs while I continue preparing the meat.'

The more his father talks about food, the less Jeanty is hungry.

'Can't we send the housekeeper?' he says, boldly.

'Finish your coffee, take the basket, and go to the village.'

When he heads back into Malmaison, Jeanty notices that the hands of the grandfather clock are still stopped at the hour of his mother's death.

&

At the market, the nut merchant hands him a cone of warm chestnuts, and, suddenly, little Jeanty is holding Pampelune's hand with a whole soft chestnut stuffed in his tiny child's mouth.

'I'll take a packet of pistachios, shelled, please.'

When she bends down to plunge her hand into the barrel, he discovers spring in her bustline. Charmed by the young lady, Jeanty is suddenly quite warm. All the snow melts in the wink of an eye. A blissful smile on his lips, he walks away from the fire where the chestnuts are roasting and heads to the butcher's.

'Monsieur, you've forgotten your pistachios!' she says, sampling a few. 'Oh! They are nice and crunchy! Plump and tasty, just the way I like them!'

The tender green of the nuts on the pink of her perfectly formed mouth … Rather than old stone manors, Poedras should paint her.

Being at the butcher's is like being at the hospital. Everything is white and red: the store's sign, the butcher's apron, the medallions of meat, and the slice of lard wrapped around them, tied with a cord.

'A veal trotter and sheep's tongues, please.'

With his cleaver, the butcher cuts the leg of the animal he is preparing and cries, 'Am I dreaming or is that Jeanty?'

'It's me, back from the Hauts-Pays!'

The perfect excuse for a quick drink in the backroom, where the renderer is hanging the carcasses.

'How is the castrated donkey doing?' he asks, toiling away. 'And your father?'

'One is preparing boar, the other has a coagulated crotch.'

The butcher hands him a slice of pliant lard.

'Take a bit of rind to seal the jaw stitching when closing the head. And go see the cep merchant; she'll give you truffles to fill the eye sockets.'

The cep merchant is sitting behind a little booth, Rita and her Jésuite pastries to her left, Odette and her tarts to her right. An infant is sleeping in one of the wicker baskets and, from another, a pile of mushrooms spills onto the gravel. A sign says she sells kisses to help sick kids. Jeanty approaches.

'Two truffles and a kiss.'

'I recognize the blue of your eyes ... You're the father's son! It's been a while!'

'Yes, it's me.'

'Then the second kiss is free, and I'll throw in a bouquet of aromatic herbs to perfume the salpicon!'

She buries her tongue in the back of Jeanty's throat and sucks on his teeth.

'Now, taste this amanita,' she whispers in his ear. 'It's called a death cap.'

Jeanty blushes; the words jump around in his head like checkers. The mushroom has a milder taste than its name suggests.

'Don't forget to glaze the head with egg whites before serving. Take a tray of chanterelles, on the house. And give my regards to your father.'

Following the sound of chirping to get the eggs, Jeanty climbs the stairs to the aviary, where young chicks in every colour are peeping loud enough to pierce his eardrums. The smell of their droppings permeates the lime mortar, and it is as if someone has sprinkled chalk in his lungs. The man who is opening and closing the doors to the little cages, adding water and grain, studies Jeanty's sophisticated-looking moiré frock coat. A peacock would suit him, but he doesn't have any. He offers him a singing nightingale.

'I would like a mining bird.'

'Mining?'

'Yes, like people say, a "mining horse."'

'Oh, a canary!'

'It's to send into a manor as a scout.'

'It will go to die in the hearth.'

'I'll take it anyway.'

'Pay me in pistachios.'

Noticing the vendor's arm covered in droppings, Jeanty suppresses a gag. Next on his shopping list: eggs and stale bread for the bread crumbs.

He stops a moment in front of the large still to watch alcohol being made. The smell of warm apples has always reminded him of the jennies' urine.

The baker immediately recognizes little Jeanty, now a young man. How is it that he feels like a stranger among all these people who watched him grow up?

'I gave all my bread crumbs to the bird vendor. Take these crusts and grate them.'

The egg woman doesn't recognize Jeanty. She offers him quail eggs at a premium.

'They're for my father,' he says, holding out some notes.

She rolls her eyes to indicate her exasperation.

'I know. When he cooks, he puts on a big show. And the resemblance is pretty hard to miss, right?'

A truck speeds by, tearing down the hill, squealing its brakes. Where did that maniac come from?

'It's a busker, a petty thief. They're taking over the streets of Noirax,' the egg lady complains.

She takes the notes and hands him the speckled eggs in a carton. He can hear her grinding her teeth. When she talks about young people, she calls them 'degenerates.'

Jeanty retraces his steps, following the aroma of roasted chestnuts.

'Back so soon?' the nut vendor says, and her laughter cracks the hazelnut shells.

'Yes, I traded my pistachios for a bird … I need more.'

Jeanty notices her chubby hands, her thick ankles, and her bulging belly. Well fed in her thatched cottage.

'I'll trade you the chestnuts for a kiss,' she whispers in his ear.

He buries his tongue in the vendor's mouth to tickle her uvula; she swallows his lips and then licks his chin. Odette looks off to the right; Rita to the left. Decidedly, Berthoumieux junior is no longer a puff pastry.

Hé, boule de gomme!	*Hey! Gumdrop!*
Serais-tu devenu un homme?	*When will you become a man?*

At the door to his shop, the butcher offers him one for the road. There is more red than white on his apron, handprints and scarlet splatters, a big blackish stain as if something exploded and sprayed. He looks like he has been shot in the stomach. Suddenly, Jeanty feels dizzy and stumbles.

'This mushroom is nicknamed the death cap,' the cep merchant had said. The last thing he sees as he collapses is the hesitant colour of the skies of Noirax, the convergence of grey, brown, and purple: a sepia sky.

☙

In this family from the Noirax bourgeoisie, the fathers are one and the same. The only difference is their choice of livestock, which is how you tell them apart. There was the Buffalo Father, the Passenger Pigeon Father, the Sheep Father, and the Donkey Father. To vary their menus, each father would occasionally dip into the abundant stock of boars and hares, without decimating the lines. Each father was conquered by his desiderata, then replaced by a son. The mothers became either thundering or transparent, self-effacing matrons.

All the Berthoumieux fathers and their descendants have eyes that are the cracked blue of a frozen lake. Blue like a black hole of loneliness. They give rabbit muffs to the women they desire, master the art of cooking stew and heads, hunt with a bow, and collect cufflinks. Sophisticated ladykillers, with handlebar moustaches, all are a little obtuse. They have the old-fashioned charm of lace collars, porcelain cups, kaolin plates, frock coats, and cameos. All the Berthoumieux fathers are the same interchangeable man.

'Come on, get up, Jeanty. It's your father. Drink a little; it'll do you good.'

Jeanty sits up, embarrassed, and takes another gulp. The basket of mushrooms has spilled on the ground, a few quail eggs have broken, the canary box has opened, and the little bird has flown away.

'We'll have to buy another canary, Father.'

'From where? What are you talking about?'

In the aviary, the bird seller has been replaced by a young girl who plays the harp, her little sister at her side. The sister turns the pages of music. Both are wheat-blond with delicate wrists, high cheekbones, and flesh exposed for all to see.

'Where did the bird seller with the arms streaked with droppings go? And the egg lady? And the busker in the van?' Jeanty asks, rubbing his temples.

'Son, you're hallucinating. Pull yourself together. Did the young cep merchant give you one of her death caps? It's not your fault; that hussy hoodwinked you … Sit down on this bench; I'm going to stop at the post office and then we'll go home to stitch up the head.'

Sing, nightingale, sing, with your heart so gay …

The voice of the fungi picker rises up in the middle of the day. *Your heart is full of laughter. Mine is full of tears.* She is nursing her baby as she croons. Her gestures and velvety voice escape neither the father nor the son. The father offers a smile, which the beguiler meets with a scowl.

A letter awaits the father at the post office.

'Just came in today,' the clerk informs him.

There is no stamp; it was hand delivered to the Berthoumieuxs' pigeonhole. The envelope bears a seal in cinnabar wax stamped with an A. The father unseals it, using the newly sharpened blade of his pocketknife. 'I will be arriving shortly, and I am hungry. I would like you to feed me. There isn't so much as a crust left at the bottom of my satchel. I am gnawing on the leather of my gloves. Let me drink straight from the bottle of your vin de pays. Slaughter an animal for me. Spray its blood on the ground, and I will sow grace in your field. Do not speak to me as I devour your beast. Do not touch me if I sleep. Fill my glass to the brim and make sure it is never empty, hold out the bottle for me to drink from, pour the wine down my throat. A new reign begins with me.'

'She speaks like an empress!'

A second picture, of the farmer in overalls, slips out of the envelope, this time in colour. He notices the paleness of her arms, the curve of her breast. And that mischievous look that invites every form of licence ... 'She is naked under her overalls,' the father thinks. 'I want this woman, and I shall have her!'

Walking back through the market in the opposite direction, the father and son greet all the vendors. Now that they know the Berthoumieuxs are preparing the head, everyone offers advice.

The baker: 'Line the edge of the dish with crusts before dressing it to soak up the melting fat. Remember to collect the suet, and don't let it burn.'

Rita: 'You need to wrap the head in cheesecloth starting at the snout. Tuck the knot in one of the nostrils and you're all set!'

The cep merchant: 'Stuff my truffles deep into the eye sockets!'

Odette: 'Veal trotter looks nice and all, but there isn't enough collagen in the cartilage. I add a sheet of gelatin.'

The renderer: 'Before serving, you need to attach the tusks, which you will have sawn off before skinning the head … At least I hope!'

The butcher: 'Eat the marrow from the bones of the head with a small spoon like camembert at room temperature.'

The charming hazelnut merchant: 'Insert shelled pistachios in the quartered tongue, which you lard before cooking.'

Even the harpist and her little sister trip over one another speaking: 'Plunge a spray of samphire in the salpicon bouillon!' They burst into champagne-bubble laughter, and the musician sounds a *la* with the tip of her index finger.

The father loves it when young ladies boss him around.

⅌

Once back on the estate, Jeanty hesitates, lingering in the doorway of Malmaison. He has a feeling that if he enters, he will also enter the Poedras painting and return to his childhood, before he began trying on perfume and dresses in secret. Maybe he will go back to the time before the fathers and their desideratas, to the spring of children's songs, both innocent and cruel.

Dans le manoir il y a un mur	*In the manor there is a wall*
Sur le mur il y a une toile	*On the wall there is a painting*
Sur la toile il y a une maison	*On the painting there is a house*
Devant la maison il y a un homme	*Before the house there is a man*

| Qui hésite à entrer | Who hesitates to go in |
| Immobile sur le seuil | Who is frozen on the threshold |

Jeanty turns and goes to hide in the woods, making it as far as his mother's headstone.

| L'arbre est dans ses feuilles | The tree is in the leaves |
| Pampelune est dans la terre | Pampelune is in the ground |

Something has changed around the estate. It is as if the chlorophyll in the foliage is denser. The centipedes have left their holes and are parading their ugliness for all to see. Blackbird eggs have hatched; fragments of blue shell fallen to the ground suggest the fine patina of kaolin. It is as if all the forest animals, from the mole to the deer and the bear, have given birth in the last twenty-four hours. A finely tuned ear can hear whimpers, whines, and moans. And the watchful eye notes, on the trail, a woman's footprints.

There is something extraordinary in the forest of Noirax. From the melting snow to the falling leaves, all the varieties of mushrooms, herbs, and flowers grow in abundance without drying up, indifferent to calendars or almanacs. Animals reproduce here more than anywhere else. The groves are streaming with the mucus of animals and the semen of males. The air meanders gently like a neck revealed, the curve of the small of the back, exaggerated to please the eye. In the forest, desire swells, puffs up, and distends, as does the wish to bloom and procreate.

The earth in Noirax has started to tremble. The water from the stream runs faster. There is rustling in the wings; Aliénor is about to enter. The forest feels her advance.

⁕

The father is in the outdoor shower, shielded from view by a low stone wall. Sliding the bar of black soap over his skin, down his torso, and toward his abdomen, he thinks back to the photo, imagines Aliénor's hand, her slender fingers on callused palms used to working on the farm and making hay, tries to glimpse her contemplative face, to recall her lewd gaze, her impish smile. The ivy, stirred by the humidity, clings to the walls with its heart-shaped leaves, in a plenitude that is also a hymn to fertility, to buzzard eggs hatched in the high branches of the hemlock, to the little worms wriggling in the humus of his wife's tomb. The worm feeds the shrew, which feeds the hare, which feeds the bird of prey, which beats its wings in the great fresco of the sky. Before such grace, humans content themselves with stumbling, blundering, spreading their dirt and scraps wherever they go. They could be removed from history, the way the artist Poedras removed them from many of his paintings, and let nature be restored. The donkey does not need the father's hands to be born, nor the rose the gardener's science to bloom. The grace of a piglet galloping toward the wallow, a flight of fireflies, and all the aromatic plants that perfume the forest air. Humans arrive in this scenery they are unworthy of, turning their neglect into theatre. If this forest is a dream, at least they will have invented words to inhabit it.

The father rubs mint leaves on his gums. The head has been cooking for a few hours. He will go pick some fruit, a pear or a peach, and slip it into the boar's mouth to make it look nice. Attach the tusks as the renderer reminded him to do.

Quick! He has to hurry, because she is approaching! She will soon set foot on the land of the Berthoumieux estate.

The Era of the Hoof and fallow land is drawing to a close; the estate will once again be sown.

May this female come with a parade of animals in her wake!

એ૩

The sound of footsteps. The father jumps.

It is only the harridan, back from the forest with a bouquet of wildflowers; she has come at his request to lay an elegant table. He hopes she didn't see the bouquet of lavender set in his undershorts on the chair earlier, but, seeing her grimace, he suspects she has. She picks off the ugly slugs that are sliming the lettuce, chops the wild garlic, puts the cheese under the bell to bring it to room temperature, salts and sugars a tomato, douses the apricots in sherry.

Jeanty tucks into a warm country loaf, ripping out the soft centre to let it melt on his tongue. He keeps the crust in a burlap napkin for the black swan he spotted at the lake during his walk.

Except that there is no swan in Noirax. Even less so a black one. Get a hold of yourself, Jeanty. Back to reality.

After wrapping the head in cloth, the father ties it with string, attached from snout to neck, so the head keeps its shape. He goes down to the cellar to select a few bottles, plunges a magnum of champagne into crushed ice. The house smells good, the aroma of head meat. The father's gaze glances over the harridan's behind without lingering. His heart beats a furious polka.

When the head is ready, it is taken out of the oven. It looks like the war-wounded, collapsed on a stretcher. Untie it. Stuff truffles in its eye sockets, straighten the hoary ears, shove a pear in the animal's mouth, present the head as is the practice. The tongue was carefully worked by the father's hand and lard melted in its pores to close the long incision where the pistachios were inserted. The head is set on an oval of soft bread. The father, in the mood for a glass of chartreuse, goes back down to the cellar.

Suddenly, the sound of a great crash on the main floor.

The harridan has knocked over a chair.

Between the painting by Poedras and the grandfather clock stopped at Pampelune's time of death, Jeanty falters. He looks like he has seen her ghost.

In the doorframe, Aliénor smiles impishly. She watches the father for a moment, as he devours her with his eyes, then admires the festive piece of meat, the tongue hanging out the side of the mouth like a lech before he cums. She grabs a silver spoon and scrapes the boar's glazed forehead, which the harridan delicately drizzled with butter. She throws back the father's glass of chartreuse, salutes her hosts, and sits at the head of the table, facing the boar's head, in the patriarch's seat.

From the forest, a voice slips in through the window and whispers in her ear things only she can hear.

Aliénor makes her entrance to Noirax.

Go on, eat, gorge yourself. Guzzle the champagne, bite the warm pear, sink your teeth into the flesh, slurp up the burning fat.

Take everything the horn of plenty places on your fork and thank no one.

You are at home here. Welcome to Malmaison.

III

LET'S GO FOR A WALK
IN THE WOODS

liénor spent four nights in the dormant building. She is the sacrificed canary. Last night, they feasted again, drank plenty of vin de pays, and even sang.

Ils m'ont appelée: Vilaine!	*They called me ugly!*
Avec mes sabots	*In my clogs*
Dondaine, oh! Oh! Oh!	*Oh! Oh! Oh!*
Avec mes sabots	*In my clogs*

After sleeping like a stone statue, she wakes up in the Perfume House mid-afternoon. Within its musty walls, behind the glass of a walnut armoire, small bottles representing a decade of perfumery are lined up. Aliénor plans to go walk in the forest for the pleasure of bursting puffballs. The night before, when she crossed her feet on the table, she saw the men frantically eye her ankle. The father in particular. But nothing scares her; she will force them into submission. Blood is stronger than milk. She is in Noirax to end the chaos, to restore order to the world.

The father will have to bow down before her. He will realize that she is running the show now, until the truth becomes clear, and victory – thunderous, white-hot – is declared, its fruit tasted.

When she thinks of Jeanty, she hears *gentil* – French for *nice* –
and finds that the name suits him. A vein pulses on his forehead
when he wants to speak but doesn't dare; he is endearing, with
something a bit elusive about him. She feels that he is hiding
something under the layer of nice. She would like to penetrate the
mystery, better understand his nature.

When the father left yesterday, Jeanty showed her the painting
that depicts Malmaison. In a hushed tone, he said he hates how
the painting makes him dizzy.

He doesn't like reality to be twisted. He doesn't like Poedras's
paintings, how he changes the direction of the ivy to appear enig-
matic. He thinks the painting is fit for the attic. One day, he will
sell it. He will have to sell Malmaison too: you can't have one
without the other.

'But Jeanty, it's your home!'

'You don't know how to look, Aliénor.'

'And you look too closely.'

Jeanty's teeth are so dazzling you can see your reflection in
their enamel. Aliénor would like to touch his tiny Adam's apple
with the tip of her index finger and say 'boop!' It's hard to tell how
old he is … Sixteen? Twenty? His energy is young. The night
before at dinner in Malmaison, Jeanty was wearing a white-and-
blue-striped sweater with an open neck that revealed the top of
his hairless torso. She is convinced that his flesh would bounce
when slapped. She looks at him and thinks: 'Alouette, je te plumerai,
I will pluck you.'

From her room in the Perfume House, Aliénor watches as
Jeanty heads toward the mouth of the forest, as its lips part to let
him in. She hopes he will look back and notice her.

Naked in the window, she offers up her creamy skin, her arched
silhouette, her defined abdominals, her patch of thick, violet down.

She would like him to come get her, to pursue her. But Jeanty continues on his way, walking merrily toward the woods, without glancing in her direction, while already the father is longing.

In the other house, also naked in the window, dick in hand, the father waits until Aliénor looks up at him. What does he have to offer? Power and protection, the charm of greying temples, the apex of attractiveness that some men reach just before their decline. A burst of sensuousness, ephemeral as glory.

She pretends she doesn't see him. It's too easy with the father; hunting by stalking is much less exciting. She would have preferred a player of her calibre who would warm up a bit before moving on to attack, savouring the euphoria of conquest even more, the glee of the moment of tearing flesh, pantsing the eel, until warm liquids spurt from the body.

Jeanty reaches the edge of the woods and disappears. His loss.

She draws the curtain and goes to wash her favourite dress, dirty with sweat and still wrinkled from long hours on the train.

It is 3:06 in the afternoon; she would like the housekeeper to make her coffee and toast with last night's lard and a bit of mustard. The ogress is hungry for all that lives, bleeds, sighs, and dies around her.

❧

After the harridan has left, while Jeanty is walking in the woods and the father is strutting through the village, Aliénor goes into Malmaison. She goes upstairs to collect information about her hosts. The freshly oiled handrails on the staircase, the waxed wooden floor: the house is well maintained. Jeanty's bedroom looks like a child's, with flashy posters of rugby teams and adventure novels. But the smell that hangs in the air is that of a man. Aliénor slips under his sheets, smells his pillow, breathes in, breathes in deep enough to rupture her bronchioles.

'I know what you do under the covers. One day, I will do things to you that at this moment you don't even know exist, as you wander like a doe through the forest. You pick sweet wild strawberries and slip a blackberry on your fingertip. The purple juice runs off your lips. You call for your mother, whimpering. I will arouse such desire in you that you will have to change your first name from Jeanty – nice. You will frighten yourself, you will enjoy yourself, you will be led astray, and you will learn to like it, knowing it cannot last forever. Nostalgia will come crashing down on you. Then you will learn to fear me, to never leave your fate in the hands of *He who observes us from on high without ever giving us a taste of our own medicine.* Together we will empty your father's wine cellar, knock back his treasures. I will be wicked. I will open your eyes. And then you will reveal your true nature.'

The décor in the father's huge bedroom is outdated. His back window looks out on the front of the Perfume House, while the three dormers offer a view over Noirax, its hill, the village, the vineyards, the little bridge, the nicely trimmed sycamore trees, and the presbytery in the distance. The father thinks of himself as a seigneur; he revels in the memory of a bygone time. *Still Life, Nude Woman at the Fountain, The Flight of Geese, The Fire of an Old Forge, Bountiful Chaos of an English Garden* … the paintings hanging on the walls are all signed *Poedras*. This bedroom is a small art gallery.

The harridan has been in here, and she will be again. She has changed the bedsheets. She rushes, she rushes, the harridan. The folds are perfect, the father's smell impossible to detect, so Aliénor opens the door to the wardrobe and breathes in the armpits of a linen shirt. She is searching for the masculine odour beneath the musky perfume. When she finds it, the fragrance speaks to her, talks dirty in her ear, of things that speak of the flesh, plump fruit, sticky loins.

'I will make this man crazed with desire. He will become a virgin again for me; I will resurrect him as I pervert his son. I will be his final spring, his infatuation, his desiderata. When I am hurt, he will kneel before me, lick my wound, nurse me, and then dissolve into tears in my skirts, like a teenager who has lost sight of himself. That is how it is. I bring all that I am and leave the arrogance of a new order in my wake.'

She would like the father to find her dozing in his bed, lolling about in his things. She wants him to be stirred by her bare shoulder, to lose his grip, his panache, and his privilege. She wants him to hurt. 'That is what I ask of him; I will coerce him and take everything he has.'

She would like to rip out his heart with pliers and petrify it with black wax so she can brandish it to the skies of Noirax in a sacrificial gesture. Then let the waxed heart rot in winter, trampled by the hoofs of jennies, soiled by the piss of boars, half gnawed by a scavenger. A moribund, despoiled heart that will feed the roots of a horn tree, a green fairy sitting on its only branch.

S'il fleurit, je serai reine	*If it blossoms, I'll be queen*
Avec mes sabots	*In my clogs*
Dondaine, oh! Oh! Oh!	*Oh! Oh! Oh!*
Avec mes sabots	*In my clogs*
En passant par Lorraine	*While passing through Lorraine*

'I will enter him by force, I will violate his privacy in Malmaison. Later, I will take possession of the land and occupy it as I see fit.

'I will drink up their memories, I will annihilate their name. I will break their line. I will leave the manor in ruins. I will rip it all up and take them both.'

o stir things up, get the old people's hips moving, and gather the young, the father organizes a dance in the village. He has rented the church basement, where the old ladies hold bingo and bazaars. The innkeeper will tend bar; Odette and Rita will work the cloakroom. He isn't sure about the music: hire a minstrel to lead the festivities or ask the pretty harpist and her sister? The second option is to his liking, but less festive. He will ask Aliénor what she thinks. That woman has an opinion on everything.

He thinks back to the feasts of recent days, to the perfection of the glaze on the boar. When she arrived, Aliénor was famished, she devoured everything, making noise with her ruby red mouth, drinking so fast and with such eagerness that the red wine dripped off the tip of her chin. She told all sorts of tales that just couldn't be, legends from her part of the country, perhaps Saud, featuring animals fornicating with other species, creating new creatures that would not survive. At the end of the meal, when it was late, they both went outdoors, the father carrying a bunch of black grapes. Aliénor sat on the porch, and he slipped a grape in her mouth, then another. They didn't speak, and the grapes burst. The young woman did not take her eyes off the father. Dawn approached, the bunch of grapes was digested, a flock of geese could be heard with their horn-like honking, followed by the first chord at the piano.

At the end of the piece, they each withdrew to their quarters. Him, naked in his large bed, with his fatigue and his fantasies. Her, kept awake by the impetuosity that guides her passions, including this mad idea to infiltrate Noirax to hunt down the truth.

❧

Perched on the hill, above the neighbour's vineyard, Jeanty observes the Jorle windmill, its pretty basin and immobilized blades. Enough is enough. Thistles and brambles have started to cover the stone; not one drop runs into the ravine. The father claims to have his hands full with Malmaison, its stubborn donkeys, the partridge hunt … Manual labour like grinding wheat and rye are less suited to his nature, but now Jeanty is here to help and wants to make himself useful. He would have liked his mother to be proud of him.

On the road back to Malmaison, he is still thinking of her.

A stranger has penetrated the Perfume House; it is not in the order of things. He preferred when the house was empty, a little sanctuary where he could pray to Pampelune and a mausoleum for her perfumes. It is no place to house the living, particularly not Aliénor, who lives more intensely than other people. And will you look at that, here she is, humming as she arrives.

Nous n'irons plus au bois, les lauriers sont coupés
La belle que voilà ira les ramasser
Si la cigale y dort, ne faut pas la blesser
Le chant du rossignol viendra la réveiller

We will go to the woods no more, the laurels have been cut
The beauty will go to gather them
If the cicada is sleeping there it must not be hurt
The nightingale's song will awaken it

She pretends to be all innocent with her stories of cut laurels, rosebush flowers, and sleeping cicadas, but her devilry and her husky voice are at odds with the innocence of the words she sings. Jeanty can barely meet Aliénor's eye because he feels like she can see through him, find the hem of a dress, a bit of skirt sticking out. 'Come,' she suggests. 'Let's go for a walk in the woods while the wolf isn't there.'

They head into the lush groves, amid trees that have stood for a century. Her eyes trained on the treetops, Aliénor doesn't watch where she is going and steps on a clump of morels, the pearl of the woods. What a waste! It's almost as if she did it on purpose. If she isn't careful, a trap will snap shut on her pretty ankle. She walks with a nonchalance that suggests that she has not often walked in the forest, where stealth is essential. She wants to spot a doe or even a she-wolf, but with all the noise she is making, there is no way an animal will cross their path, aside from a stupid coypu.

At the stream, when she bends down to drink, her long hair dangles in the water. Suddenly, a bird emits a cry that sounds like a meow. A buzzard swoops down on a young hare, clutches it in talons, carries it off into the skies. Aliénor notices nothing of the spectacle of life killing to survive. She sees the forest with less acuity than human faces, as if her thoughts were sailing on other waves. Is she from the Hauts-Pays, Finistax, Saud, or Ouestan?

'I don't answer questions about where I'm from.' She dodges the inquiry and grows sad.

A cloud passes over their heads. She pulls a flask from her pocket, takes a swig, and holds it out toward Jeanty's mouth, as he suppresses a gag, but she forces him to drink anyway. The fiery decoction burns his taste buds and makes him dizzy. He makes a face, and she laughs at him. He finds her brusque; she finds him … nice. And a bit boring, truth be told. This walk is lacking in danger.

'Jeanty, tell me one of your secrets,' she commands.

'I am not who you think I am.'

She bursts out laughing, then lunges at him as if to kiss him, but grabs his golden curls and pulls him toward her. There is something coarse about this girl. Aliénor is indelicate in nature, almost virile.

'I could pierce your ears,' she offers, pinching them. 'Both or just one, as you like.'

Aliénor's peppery breath, her lack of modesty and good manners, disconcert him, but he doesn't fear her, or desire her. Is it because her face is ethereal and her features angelic, despite the wicked glint in her blue eye? Her walleyed gaze – one eye a soft black, the other streaked with a flame of blue – unsettles him a little too much not to want her.

'Now it's your turn to tell me a secret,' Jeanty challenges her once she releases her hold.

'I'm not who you think I am either.'

She asks whether he knows the names of the herbs that grow in the forest of Noirax. The creeping rosemary doesn't interest her, nor the wild garlic, or the sage. She is not moved by the perfect oval of the thick fiddleheads. She is not telling him everything, and Jeanty feels like he is getting the runaround.

'Tell me which herbs you are looking for, and I will tell you whether we have them here.'

'I've forgotten their names.'

Watching Aliénor rummage through the woods, wearing her damp, wrinkled dress, with her dark hair and her look impossible to decipher, a clear intuition comes to him: this woman is going to be the cause of their ruin.

'Quit teasing and give me some hints at least!'

'The green fairy eats them.'

'What are you playing at, Aliénor?'

'There are six of them. The first herb looks like lavender, and its leaves are grouped in an ear. It has antiseptic properties. You find it in the gardens of priests ... It is named in a passage of the Bible.'

Jeanty perks up and recites from memory:

'And you shall take a bunch of hyssop and dip it in the blood that is in the basin, and touch the lintel and the two doorposts with the blood that is in the basin.'

'Yes, that's it, it's hyssop! Oh! Jeanty! You're incredible!'

Satisfied, he leads her to a hyssop shrub. Its purple flowers with their citrus scent thrive in the shade and the coolness of stones. Aliénor picks a few sprays, stops, and looks around with a strange glint in her eyes, apprehension in her voice.

'Where are we?' she asks, suddenly more serious.

'On my mother's grave.'

Crouched in the dense thicket, the harridan spies on them. Decidedly, these two dimwits are playing mighty strange games, taking risks without knowing it. She disapproves of Jeanty's reck-lessness and temerity. You don't walk on hallowed ground the way you do on the farm or at the market! Since they broke down the door of the Perfume House, anything is possible again, and they will see where it ends up. This young woman brings fever with her. The harridan feels something tighten in her chest.

he father returns from the post office, his arms filled with a box and several letters. As he enters Malmaison, he immediately notices the bouquet of wild herbs set in the centre of the table: purple hyssop and veronica sprays, sprigs of lemon balm, the tender green of fennel, and the yellow buttons of wormwood.

'All I need is anise, and I'll be able to boil up a first batch of spirits!' Aliénor announces excitedly. 'Isn't it wonderful?'

The father starts. He didn't expect the production of absinthe to be organized so quickly. Nor to find Aliénor in the main building of the estate without an invitation. There is brief silence, then an exclamation of enthusiasm.

'It's extraordinary! I told you you can find anything in the forest!'

Aliénor rips open the box brought back from the post office inscribed with her name and the word FRAGILE. It contains several carefully wrapped objects in blown glass and old pieces of metal. There are goblets, slotted spoons in the shape of leaves, some of the parts for a still.

'The green fairy!' she cries, filled with emotion.

Arms raised to the sky, a woman arches her winged back to lift a crystal ball mounted with four thin brass taps. The father has before him a genuine absinthe fountain.

'We will have several reasons to celebrate in the village!' he cries.

'A party? Wonderful! I'll need a new dress!'

Aliénor jumps from desire to desire, from a fountain to a fairy to a forest to a dress to a man to an animal to a mushroom to the heart of a bird. She is hard to please, but life beats so strongly in her that one can't help but want to burn one's fingers from contact with her.

'There are bolts of silk, fabrics from Asia, and a piece of serge in the attic. The harridan will make you a new one!'

As he opens his letters, the father stiffens. Yet more clowns wanting to fleece him! He will have to see to this matter, hone his image and burnish his reputation, if he wants to keep expanding his influence. The matter is becoming more urgent. The father dreams, more and more openly, of making a leap into politics. Municipal to start with, then he will see. Born to rule, that's how he sees himself. He likes an expansive horizon. He always has to head off the beaten path, as far off as possible.

The harridan's bovine shoulder forces the trapdoor that leads to the attic. A diaphanous veil floats in the room, and the air is dryer than expected. A mouse scurries past to hide under the vanity, which contains Pampelune's things. A jewellery box, a kimono collection, a pair of purple ankle boots with black beading, a woman's large hat, a collection of romance novels, a compact mirror, a large pink shell open like a mouth crying for help, a marble knick-knack in the shape of a goddess brought back from a honeymoon in the Cyclades, and, in a frame, a portrait of a mother and child.

A tarp hides the old Singer sewing machine with bolts of fabric lined up beside it. There is an iron mannequin to hang dresses in the making. Everything has its place in a sewing basket with a fox-hunting motif: thread, buttons, tape measure, scissors, bobbins, needles.

The harridan unrolls a metre of lace for a slip around Aliénor's hips, notes the measurements of her body. This close, Aliénor's charm strikes in the middle of the chest. Next to her, you enter the circle of fire and want to sing with her, catch the fever. You want to hurt her or be hurt by her. Marking the seams for the waist, the harridan grazes her with the needle. A tiny drop of blood appears on the young woman's flank, and the harridan orders her to stop moving.

In the sunbeam that comes in through the dormer, Aliénor notices that fine down covers the face of the woman who is sewing. 'The skin on your cheek is fuzzy like a sage leaf,' she notes, supressing a mad laugh.

The needle nips her flesh again. Again and again, like petit-point embroidery, hurting her in a series of shocks. The pain surprises Aliénor, and a tear rolls down her face.

In a corner of the room, a cage holds the memory of a carrier pigeon. The harridan hums softly that in the bird there was a heart.

Le coeur est dans l'oiseau	*The heart is in the bird*
L'oiseau est dans l'oeuf	*The bird is in the egg*

Near the spinning wheel there is a second iron mannequin. The train of a wedding dress sticks out from under its cover. Another grey mouse escapes from it.

L'amour est dans la femme	*The love is in the woman*
La femme est dans la robe	*The woman is in the dress*
Mais la robe est un linceul	*But the dress is a shroud*
Le linceul est dans la terre	*The shroud is in the ground*

The two women sing together louder and louder, increasingly out of tune. There is something in this off-key song that is like revealing a family secret or making a statement to the police. The confessions fall into the void, because there is no one to receive them. Only the judgement of *He who is perched on high*, ever ready to let the blade of blame drop on the little people who are falling, erring, stumbling.

few years ago, when Jeanty was fourteen, one night when his father was sleeping, the boy went up to the attic and found a large oval mirror on legs. His reflection in the cheval glass disgusted him. The resemblance to his father was settling in. In addition to the eye colour and the aquiline nose, the distinctive facial features of the Berthoumieux clan were starting to take over the softness of those of Pampelune. The fuzz above his lip, the increasingly square shoulders, the broader trapezius muscle and, above all, that slightly moronic je-ne-sais-quoi that the Berthoumieux fathers display in their portraits – all these attributes were emerging in him. It was undeniable, the transformation had begun: he was starting to look like his father.

Not being able to take any more, Jeanty turned the cheval glass around.

What he discovered on the other side of the mirror filled him with wonder.

Before being transformed into a cheval glass, the oval piece of caramel pine had served as a frame. In the sculpted wood on the other side of the reflection, a Poedras painting was lodged – perhaps his most beautiful. Entitled *Mother and Child*, the portrait depicted a young Pampelune in a blue dress holding a cherub against her breast.

Jeanty then liberated said blue dress from its protective cover and dared to put it on, adding stones and pearls at his neck. When he looked at himself in the cheval glass, he liked his new image, and kissed it. Through the mouth of the shell set on the vanity among the maternal relics, an imaginary lover whispered words that cheered him and made him sneeze. 'Yes, I do.' Jeanty gave his consent.

Hidden from the world and its mockery, he spread his arms a little to make the dress billow. The shadow projected on the wall was that of a holy icon, and blond curls formed a halo around his forehead.

'Hail Mary full of grace, pray for me and forgive my trespasses. Now and at the hour of my death, but particularly now …'

In his head, a voice answered that he was blessed among all women and that the fruit of his womb would be blessed as well.

aily life in the household was reorganized once the young people arrived on the estate. The harridan is required every day for meal preparation and housekeeping. Jeanty accompanies his father on missions that the father keeps inventing to sound out the electors, to find out what the villagers are dreaming of, to uncover their hopes and their fears.

Small merchants, cobblers, innkeepers, fishmongers, florists: they amass a nice little nest egg and make a living. Everyone is doing better than the father would have thought. They have thatched cottages, gondolas, and parakeets in a cage. In the summer, they find a haven in Saud, where they bake their bodies in the heat. They like it and come home refreshed. Those who make a living from the mines and the mill have been less fortunate and are crammed together in small, humble cottages. They have the same wants: fresh meat (but they won't have it) and growing richer (but it won't happen). The representatives of the little people who speak at town meetings fear for the future of their offspring. What will their children live on if the village sits idle? This is what keeps them up at night. The blades of the mill have stopped fanning the air. The kaolin reserves have been exhausted. They don't track small game like they used to to feed themselves. Since these activities ended, the village has shrunk and ground to a halt, like a tree drained of its sap. Time has stopped in Noirax. The fields left fallow look like English gardens. Where the wheat once whipped the air, all that grows is desolation. Sometimes through the crusted mud rises up, with great struggle, a sad clump of mandrake. The mines have been abandoned. No one is seeking their fortune in rocks split, dug out, beaten by strong winds and inclement weather.

While pretty much everywhere in Noirax, the sleepiness spreads, there are people like Aliénor who claim that new cultures are possible. 'In Noirax, the horn tree will grow on the Malmaison estate,' she announced to the father. He has no idea what that means, but she looks like she knows what she's talking about.

In her veins, Aliénor feels the pressure of her blood. She walks the forest forward and back, spots herbs for her first trials, macerations, and decoctions. While waiting for the second box with the remaining parts of the still, she dries plants that will be useful, sprouts seeds for the ones she is missing, yellow worm- wood and green anise, and stumbles on a rare sort of lichen. She inadvertently invents herbal teas to make the drinker paranoid, plays with the raspberry bush and nettles, steeps the roots of the dried fern and a sugar cube in cold water, swallows shoots that leave her trembling and convulsing, alone in the Perfume House. It passes; she continues her research under the inquisitive eye of the harridan, who, upstairs at Malmaison, watches her while dusting the purple velvet curtains that hang in the father's bedroom window, stage left.

This morning, Aliénor chopped hallucinogenic herbs to cook up in an omelette. It was not a mistake; these she knows well. She stretches out in the shade of a linden tree to rest. Within the walls of the Perfume House, mould blooms and muddles her percep- tions. The house gives her no comfort. It is impossible to gather her strength here to advance the projects she has in mind.

In the ablution room, the pretty kaolin tiles in gold, ivory, and ultramarine depict the courtship of two amorous peacocks. As she lowers herself into the clawfoot bathtub, she notices, at the base of the wall, that ivy has come in through the low window that airs the room and has twisted around the foot of the portmanteau where Pampelune used to hang her kimonos with their bright colours of spice and peonies.

While she is dozing in the bathtub, a vision comes to her for the first time. Suddenly, the water takes on the odour of salt and cold metal, becomes gelatinous and heavy like mercury. Aliénor is completely submerged in pink cream: the blood of a dead woman, blended with milk.

A certainty rises to the surface: in this place, it's kill or be killed.

n Noirax, the rumour spreads like wildfire. Everyone is invited to an evening organized by the father Berthoumieux: the old, the young, the penniless, the wealthy, the powerless, and the powerful. The event will take place in the church basement, in the room where town meetings the father attends are held. The smell of old dust and petty problems reigns. The evening of the ball, the belles and the bulls arrive arm in arm, already a little tipsy. There will be thistle wine and Troussepinette, turnip and rutabaga chips for all villagers.

The father has smoothed his moustache with care, sprinkled a few drops of aftershave in his boxers, and put on his felt hat. Jeanty is dressed as an androgynous sailor. Aliénor pierced his ear and lent him a gold hoop. She has donned the dress the harridan made, a multicoloured, breathtaking, shimmering splendour, bespoke attire, designed to dazzle and induce nausea. 'Don't hide the dress's seams,' she commanded. 'Show them off!' A crown of burgundy phlox set on her shiny black hair makes her look like a despot. She will be the only one people see, and that is her goal.

As soon as he sees it, Jeanty falls in love with Aliénor's dress. The frock gives her power – or reveals the power that was stifled under the corset. This creation born of the harridan's agile hands is even more remarkable than Pampelune's blue dress. Jeanty feels an intense desire rise and wash over him: he wants to wear the dress himself, feel the fabric hug his slender boy's body. And then, maybe, see his own femininity shine through, triumphant.

For the occasion, the father has prepared the hot air balloon. 'We will travel to the village by balloon!' he trumpets. Aliénor has noticed that the father denies her nothing. The night before, she tested him: 'I would like to arrive at the party with a llama on a leash!' The father is amused by her wildest suggestions, her most theatrical eccentricities, and he sees to them personally.

The harridan sends off this improbable trio waving a little embroidered hankie. She shrinks as the balloon takes to the sky.

Piloting the balloon requires all the father's concentration. As they fly over the lands of the Centre, Aliénor becomes interested in the Jorle Mill, still standing immobile.

'It's hard to believe, but that used to be an important mill with a lovely millstone,' Jeanty says. 'An old miller and his wife lived there with their daughter, who was as beautiful as the rising sun, generous, and without malice: Pimparela.'

At this point, he has the complete attention of Aliénor, who has turned back into a little girl dressed up as a princess being read a story. Hanging on Jeanty's every word, she drinks in the tale as if it were the most exquisite nectar. Aliénor likes being told stories so she can rewrite the endings.

'Crimes were committed around here ...' Jeanty reveals, lowering his voice. Uttering the names of the places: Cache-du-Loup, Tuères, Lac du Gisant, Butte au Massacre ... 'If you've never heard the legend of Pimparela, you must be from Saud or Finistax!'

'I told you the other day, I don't answer questions about where I am from!'

Once they are told, the legends, like songs, are scattered to the wind, like disoriented pigeons. They exist in the mouths of those who tell them or set them to melody, otherwise they vanish and die.

Believing she heard a noise, the harridan descends the grand staircase. Her duster in the air, she looks around the room. At first glance, everything seems to be in its place.

In the centre of the acacia table, in a kaolin vase set on a tablecloth with a houndstooth motif, the herbs picked by Aliénor are starting to wilt. A country loaf is cooling on the bread board. On a serving platter with a wide rim, grapes, apricots, and cherries are ripening before being turned into jellies and jam. At the other end of the table, a man's clutter is tossed down any which way: letters, requests, and bills – the father's paperwork – weighted by an iron goose, a small box of catechu for fresh breath, a calculator, four old keys on a lucky rabbit's foot keychain, a few old bent nails, two pictures of Aliénor at the farm, and a pile of pamphlets for the father's campaign.

Lurking behind the eternal objects, the harridan is convinced that something has changed. Is it the smell of the stagnant water for the flowers? A burnt-out lightbulb that makes things look different? She holds her breath and advances cautiously toward the Poedras painting. There is something different in the painting of the manor. She notices that a detail has just been added to the canvas: at the window of the spouses' bedroom, a hand draws the curtain to conceal what is happening from view.

An immense sense of unease grows inside her, heats her ears, and turns her cheeks red.

She takes a set of keys and hurries out of Malmaison.

The self-proclaimed queen, the self-proclaimed aristocrat, and the squire initiate their landing. The villagers gather and start singing that *Friday night, the king, the wife, and the little prince came to my house to shake my hand.* As the balloon starts to touch down to boisterous applause, Aliénor notices that a llama is grazing peacefully at the end of a tether.

'How darling!' she says, delighted. 'We should start raising llamas at the estate! We could have emus, too, and ostriches, and wild turkeys! It would be amazing, extraordinary! Donkeys get boring after a while.'

'Tut, tut, tut, I won't have anyone insult my jennies,' the father answers, as he executes his landing manoeuvres.

Barely out of the basket, Aliénor and Jeanty run toward the animal, which turns its slim neck toward them as it chews grass energetically with its misaligned jaws, their movement following a slightly ridiculous elliptical course. The father calls them back to him.

'Come on, kids! We're running late!'

Aliénor unhitches the leash from the stake and leads the llama along with them.

'Watch your crown, Aliénor,' Jeanty warns, 'or the llama will eat it!'

They burst out laughing and pick up the pace. Accelerating, the llama starts to amble.

In the parish hall, ready to melt into the crowd of young people who are already dancing and drinking, the father remarks that the party is a success. The low notes of a prelude vibrate in his chest. His pupils dilate and joy fills his heart. Aliénor looks around to ensure that no other woman is wearing a dress as sparkly as hers. They are dressed in muted colours, their skin is oily, and their hair is as dull as a salt lick. No one will overshadow her tonight; she will sparkle!

From high on a platform, the conductor is leading a quartet of baroque musicians.

The father joins a group of men in conversation, glasses in hand. How can they drink that plonk? He would like a drink too, but the red wine tastes like carrion, the white like medication. He holds his nose, throws back a few ounces of vodka, and is perked up, his tongue loosened and his eye full of mischief, ready to mix with the little people and talk to the voters – except for the ones with bad breath.

The sonata ends on a pianissimo to hand things over to the father. The moment has come to hold forth.

As he advances to the stage, heads turn toward the aspiring politician, and silence falls over the room. He recognizes a few faces: the renderer, his favourite merchant, the baker, the little hazelnut seller, and the innkeeper. At first, the father seems a bit nervous. After the usual niceties, he talks about life in Noirax and what prompted him to get into politics. The father expresses pride in his genealogy, reminds the villagers of the succession of fathers Berthoumieux who have prospered in Noirax. He sermonizes with fervour and conviction about the grand old days of kaolin, tantalizes the entrepreneurial fibre of those gathered. The father promises that, if he is elected, he will promote local know-how again by restarting the production of nourishing grains with the support and knowledge of Aliénor, an agricultural expert, to stem the exodus of young people toward factory towns. His son, Jeanty, will get the rotor of the mill going again and oversee its reopening. The father is charismatic and a good speaker. He quivers when applauded and grows sombre when talking about political tensions and the spectre of war. The women look him up and down blushing; some whisper that he is a widower and a catch. Others would like their daughters to marry his son. As for the men, the father makes them want to lift themselves up, to think big. He concludes by inviting the villagers to dream of a collective project, and, on this beautiful summer's evening, to let the baroque music carry them away.

The first notes of music rise in the muggy air and stir the crowd. The conductor sweeps his arms, with plenty of energy and vigour, and then the movements of a joyful piece are played. Couples form on the dance floor and start to move again. The fair ladies go this way and that way, and then it is the handsome gentlemen's turn to hop merrily to the rhythm of a piece that is in fashion but not to the father's liking.

He takes the opportunity to go get a drink. As he crosses the room, he hopes to spot Jeanty in the crowd, but doesn't see him anywhere. He is not at the bar, not in the bathroom, not on the dance floor. Outside, there are pipe smokers and a throng of soldiers in military attire. Two of them are buying laughing mushrooms from the little merchant. In the distance, the llama is grazing, supremely unaware of the madness around it. Jeanty shines in his absence.

The father checks the little kitchen where they store the cheap wine and the oil to fry the slices of turnip: his son isn't there either.

In the cloakroom, Odette and Rita knit during the lulls in the evening.

'He came by this way,' says Odette, pointing to the left.

'He will come back this way,' says Rita, pointing in the other direction.

The father goes outside, muttering. This bad wine and the music are getting the better of his patience. He takes refuge in the little chapel where a few votive candles are burning, makes the sign of the cross, alone before God and his conscience. He brings his palms together and kneels to pray. 'Make my words clear, my gestures confident, my decisions fair. And grant me the fleeting pleasures of the flesh.' The insolent laugh of a young woman interrupts his prayer. Leaving the chapel to see what is going on, he spots the flounce of a full pink skirt and approaches silently. A young lady and a pyrotechnician are kissing behind the chapel.

Enjoy it, young people, enjoy it. Bite into the apple, sink your teeth into the belly of the suckling pig, receive the treasures from the horn of plenty. Yes, this is how things should be.

In the parish hall, the soldiers twirl the young ladies. Members of the air force make the biggest impression. The confidence and arrogance of the pilots seduce the ladies, and that is how it will always be. They whisper in their ears that they will be back at Easter or Trinity, and other promises they cannot keep.

À l'entour de leur tombe	*All around their grave*
Mironton, mironton, mirontaine	*Mironton, mironton, mirontaine*
À l'entour de leur tombe	*All around their grave*
Romarin l'on plantera	*We will plant rosemary*
On verra voler leur âme	*We will see their soul take flight*
Mironton, mironton, mirontaine	*Mironton, mironton, mirontaine*
On verra voler leur âme	*We will see their soul take flight*
Au travers des lauriers	*Through the laurels*

Aliénor twirls in the middle of the dance floor so that the flounce of her dress fans out in front of the other women, who are both admiring and envious. At the end of the enchantment, hatred will have replaced fascination. Forging a path through the colours, the noise, and the agitation, the father heads toward her. Brusque bow strokes express more dramatic notes, and the crowd grows livelier. They change partners. As old hands graze Aliénor and younger ones seek out her flesh under the gathers in the dress, she takes refuge in the arms of the father and whispers something in his ear. He can't hear her and asks her to repeat it. Then she slips her tongue into his ear. Hands reach out to her again, he holds her a while longer against him, until the rhythm slows, before it takes off even faster. The light man times the lighting effects with the crescendos in the music. Cries of joy rise up from the crowd.

In the vestry, Jeanty lets himself be kissed gently by the hazelnut seller, while an infantryman gives him head. He grips the soldier's muscular shoulder. Then, as if in a game of musical chairs, they change places and roles. To the touch, the young woman's shoulder is like a ripe peach, perfect in its tenderness, ready to bite. The masculine lips find and taste each other, gluttonous, hungry. The fingers undo belt buckles and corset busks. The suits of soldier, sailor, and dauphiness are strewn on the ground. Sensitivities are revealed, preferences become clear. The rhythm of the lovemaking intensifies. And, for once, *He who observes us from on high* stops watching.

Chacun mit ventre à terre
Mironton, mironton, mirontaine
Chacun mit ventre à terre
Et puis se releva

Each man lies face down on the ground
Mironton, mironton, mirontaine
Each man lies face down on the ground
And then rises again

On the dance floor, a drunken elector charges at the father with the breath of the dying and shouts in his face that he can count on his vote. Gagging, the father leaves the room before he vomits.

He heads toward the forest, with the intention of getting lost there to recover his wits, when suddenly someone grabs him from behind.

The father has the impression that someone is trying to slit his throat like a piglet, but instead he is pushed toward the forest, away from the party.

'Aliénor, you don't need to be so rough; I'll follow you wherever you want. Relax your grip on my neck, for god's sake!'

Yes, he will follow her tracks; it's beyond his control. She holds out a mushroom to him.

'Try it,' she commands, 'and chew slowly before swallowing.'

The fireflies light up as Aliénor walks by, and the trees rustle gently, as if to seduce them, inviting them deeper into the belly of the forest. With her hand, she caresses the ferns and encourages him to do likewise. He touches the leaves, and under his fingers they transform into a delicate lace skirt. Aliénor's fanciful dress is an oil stain on the green landscape. After the llama, the dress, and the hot-air balloon, what else will she ask him for?

He will remember that, at precisely this moment, Aliénor turned to tell him they were about to slip through the looking glass.

'Come, don't be afraid,' she says, taking his hand.

After searching for his father and Aliénor in vain for a half hour at first light, Jeanty invited a few of the revellers to end the night at Malmaison. Soldiers with low morals, young gentlemen, and women of easy virtue are strewn about here and there, on the sofas in the living room, in the bedrooms, sunk into armchairs, collapsed on the thick rug, gathered in front of the Poedras painting.

In his bed, lying between the infantryman and the hazelnut vendor, Jeanty is sleeping peacefully. A light breeze comes in through the window, making the lace curtains billow and caressing the lovers' skin.

Outside, in the distance, a voice approaches.

Alouette, gentille alouette	*Lark, lovely lark*
Alouette, je te plumerai	*Lark, I will pluck you*
Je te plumerai les yeux	*I will pluck your eyes*
Je te plumerai le cou	*I will pluck your neck*
Et les ailes!	*And your wings!*
Et la queue!	*And your tail!*
Et le dos!	*And your back!*
Aaah!	*Aaah!*

Arriving at Malmaison, Aliénor comes face to face with a young man who is making coffee in the kitchen. The young squire is buck naked. 'I'll have a cup too, thank you.' She places the oyster mushrooms she picked along the way in a bowl and her harvest of lichen in the cupboard where aromatics and teas are stored.

The harridan is conspicuously absent; she turned on her heels in the early morning when she discovered the indolent young people lolling about in the manor. It is not the first time, nor will it be the last, that evil has entered Malmaison, but the harridan does not like to see libertines invade a place that is under her care.

On the staircase leading up to the second floor, Aliénor runs into soldiers in creased uniforms. The masks have fallen, and the faded women are preparing to leave, buttons in the wrong holes. Sounds come from Jeanty's bedroom: movements, whimpers, panting. Aliénor smiles. She peeks in the father's quarters: no one has been in there all night. The bed has not been slept in; the fold in the duvet is impeccable. Before dropping onto it, Aliénor walks to the window, pulls back the curtain a bit, and sees the fountain goddess – her neck, her slender waist, and the hollow of her back. In the basin, water lilies offer themselves up, open, in all their splendour, as a wet cry emerges from Jeanty's room. She recognizes the voice and is delighted; then, to make it night, draws the curtain, which falls like a velvet drape in an old theatre. Exhausted, she falls asleep in the father's bed while, in a forest not far from there, lost like Little Thumb at the end of his store of pebbles, the father advances with great difficulty. He feels air enter through his back and exit through his chest. *He loses blood from beneath his wing.*

What is he doing abandoned in the neighbouring forest, this early, naked as the day he was born? There are large gaps in his memory of the night. The ends of his moustache are pointing any which way, making him look a bit lost. A sharp pain shoots out from his back. The father goes to drink from the pond, then dives in completely.

He remembers that, at one point, as they were reaching the edge of the woods, fireworks exploded in the sky in green, purple, and silvery bouquets. Aliénor shouted: 'Come on, let's make a run for it!' Then she cursed, hearing in the distance the piece she wanted to hear. Yes, he remembers that detail. For a moment, Aliénor considered going back to the party, then changed her mind, heading further into the woods with the father.

Galvanized by the party and his speech, the father was on a roll and sought, it seemed, to make the pleasure last. No longer able to listen to him speechify, Aliénor begged him to shut up, but he continued to jabber on. So, with her characteristic brusqueness, she said something like: 'You talk like others scratch themselves, frenetically, unable to help yourself. It's maddening! Quit yapping. Your reign is ending; soon your words won't be worth as much, so you might as well get used to it.' What happened next was a muddle in the father's mind.

His back is throbbing, but he can't see the deep lacerations: two slashes to his flesh. 'I have been battered!' the father grimaces, overcome by the desire to give in to tears. While he splashes around gingerly in the pond, the harridan gets rid of any traces of the libertines' visit to Malmaison. In the father's bedroom, the curtain goes up with a mechanical squeak. Illusions and dreams touch down in the orchestra pit.

Jeanty joins Aliénor, carrying an appetizing tray of food.

'Wake up,' he says. 'You slept all afternoon. You need to eat something!'

With Aliénor's harvest, he has made an oyster mushroom and donkey chorizo crepe, with a salad of daikon greens on the side. The crust of the country loaf crackles; the butter melts on the soft bread. A few slices of Tomme and a cup of tea complete the meal.

'These mushrooms you browned with a sprig of thyme are delicious! The infusion of lichen is just for you. I picked it with you in mind. You should know one thing: it is a rare plant, between alga and fungus, which has feminizing effects on the body. It's up to you whether or not you want to drink it.'

It is as if Hansel and Gretel were devouring the walls of the gingerbread house and its sugar windows, a brother and sister conspiring while the parents are away. A new collusion has developed between them. As he drinks the lichen tea, Jeanty tells her about the filthy things he did with the tank driver and the pistachio vendor, not holding anything back, showing Aliénor his bruised knees and the raw corners of his mouth.

'How I love hearing about you getting down in the muck like that!' she exclaims, carefully refraining from telling him what she did to the father.

'It's too bad my lover is going off to war and doesn't know when he'll be back!'

Il reviendra z'à Pâques	*He'll be back for Easter*
Mironton, mironton, mirontaine	*Mironton, mironton, mirontaine*
Il reviendra z'à Pâques	*He'll be back for Easter*
Ou à la Trinité	*Or for Trinity Sunday*

'Jeanty! You have such a beautiful voice. It's a shame you don't like to sing!'

'I don't like to sing with my man's voice. But in a higher pitch, with a woman's voice, I don't mind it. If I was forced under torture to sing, I would choose a lament for all the bums and beggars who have been lost along the way.

Emmène-moi là où ça sent l'amour
Refaire mon nid, le mien s'est détruit
Emmène-moi là où ça meurt le jour
Ailleurs c'est trop loin
Beaucoup trop loin

Take me to where it smells like love
Remake my nest, mine has been destroyed
Take me to where the day dies
Somewhere else is too far away
Much too far

The melancholy of the ballad, words and music combined, is perfect for the morning after the night before, for coming down from intoxicated highs. Jeanty and Aliénor sing together.

Si je pouvais au moins voir de face
Ce que je sais, ce que je suis
J'ai quelque chose en dedans de mon coeur
Qui me fait vibrer, tout au long de moi

Aide-moi, aide-moi à me retrouver
Aide-moi, aide-moi à me retrouver

Je suis perdue, ou je suis coincée
Je suis tannée de toujours me cacher

At least if I could see head on
What I know, what I am
I have something in my heart
That makes me quiver head to toe

Help me find myself
Help me find myself

I am lost, or I am stuck
I am tired of always hiding

Someone bounds up the stairs four at a time, bursts into the bedroom, and ruins the magic of the moment.

'Your father has been wounded!' the harridan announces, breathless. 'The cep merchant found him in the woods. The renderer went to fetch him with his stretcher.'

Jeanty goes pale.

'Did he have an accident?!'

'He hurt himself … in the forest … That's all I know. We have to go get him at the renderer's and bring him back to Malmaison. Jeanty, call the doctor! Aliénor, let's boil some water and prepare sterile cloths to clean the wound.'

Aliénor clenches her jaw. Caring for the powerful, working humbly at their service and in their shadow, revolts her.

'I am not the father's maid.'

While the doctor palpates and probes him, the father moans in his bed, complains that the air is blowing through his wounds, and calls for drugs much too powerful for his condition. When the harridan bends to place a damp cloth on his burning forehead, he can't stop himself from breathing in her armpits.

The doctor asks her to leave them alone. He has the father lie on his stomach and starts disinfecting the area around the gashes. He has never had to care for this sort of wound. The father asks what they look like, and the doctor's answer surprises him.

'Like an open sex. With something inside. Were you whipped?'

'I think I was ridden,' the father confesses, a little ashamed.

The doctor's eye lights up with a bawdy glint. The upturns of his moustache rise.

'I see … Someone did things to you and it got out of hand. Did you end the evening in a brothel?' he asks, in a hushed tone.

'No, no … It happened in the forest.'

A first groove runs from the shoulder blade to the lower back. The second laceration is not as deep, but something that is not flesh is emerging from it and curls at the edge of the wound. The doctor fishes around in the gash with a small tweezer, grabs something in the shape of a ribbon and pulls, intrigued, as if it were a message in a fortune cookie.

'Mr. Berthoumieux, there is something written in the flesh of your back!'

The doctor injects an anesthetizing substance in the other wound to be able to fish around in it without making the father scream. In it, he finds a small object that looks like a baby tooth, cleans it in the metal tray with alcohol and a cotton ball, and discovers, dumbfounded, a delicate shell. He steps back, steps forward, bows his head, furrows his brow, and comes to a decision.

'I will sew you up,' he tells the father. 'You will use bath salts to help heal the wounds, and I will come to check on how they are progressing.'

'Doctor?'

'Yes.'

'What is written on my back?'

The doctor gulps down his saliva.

'Better drowned than unhappily married.'

t is not only on the Berthoumieux estate that Noirax has a twisted history with women who are desired and who desire in turn. In the village, everyone knows the legend of Pimparela and remembers, without malice, when passing by the Jorle Mill, the story of the old miller, his wife, and their young daughter.

It happened shortly after the Benedictine fathers deserted, during the Era of the Horn. At the time, there was no longer a priest in the church, nor a single nun in the convent for the education of the young ladies. One can confidently argue that this was apparent in the miller's daughter, who smiled at all passersby. Because of this, she was given the nickname of a pretty flower that grows throughout the prairies of the Centre and that anyone can take home: the pimparela, a sort of daisy.

In anticipation of proposals of marriage, the old miller had set aside a cask of wine and enough rye to get through the winter, but the days, the weeks, the months, and the seasons went by, and no one came to ask for the hand of his daughter, who remained free as the air. The villagers started to hum, 'The girl from Jorle/Whom everyone can pick/but nobody wants.'

Sorrow, anguish, jeers, and illness ended up getting the better of the miller and the miller's wife. They died before they could marry off their daughter. Plucky and hard working in adversity, Pimparela took over the family business, drowning her sorrow in work. She got the mill turning again, helped by her young neighbour, a farmhand named Jeanneton, ten years her junior. They are the ones depicted on the charcoal canvas hanging in the bedroom of the Perfume House of a horsewoman forcibly intoxicating a dazed farmhand.

Winter settled in, with its parade of viruses and fevers, taking the young man's poor mother in its wake. After a year as a widower, Jeanneton's father, a man with a menacing eye and a wandering hand, undertook to court Pimparela, who was no longer of an age to be choosy. The hour had come to say: 'Take the one you can have rather than the one you want.' The marriage was celebrated between the worn-out man and the lady miller. Their union caused the son great sadness. Rage in his heart, he enlisted in the army as a way out of Noirax.

'Better drowned than unhappily married,' whispered the matrons and the stepmothers when the grizzled, stooped father appeared at the door to the church on the arm of a woman many years younger. When the wind lifted the skirt of her dress, you could see that she was wearing garters and, between her legs, a pimparela to hide her sex. When the village idiot was hit in the head by the bouquet, he lost both his cap and his wits.

Like a broken-down horse going at a filly's hindquarters, Jeanneton's father tried to service the young woman the best he could. He lost a lot of weight, became increasingly emaciated and anemic, with a goofy smile always on his face. He told himself boorish jokes and burst out laughing while beating the rye and the oats. He thanked the heavens while confessing his sins, and, when night fell, he slept like a log, a deep sleep that was not the sleep of the righteous. After a few years of hard labour within the damp stone walls, he got sick. Barley soups, gin pumices, and mustard plasters could not get him back on his feet.

After receiving his orders, proud in his tailored soldier's uniform, Jeanneton came back to the mill to say goodbye to the married couple and show them he was doing well. His anger had passed, and he was ready to see them again. But what he found at the mill sent him into a state of despair from which he would never recover.

To get the mill going in his bedridden father's absence, Pimparela turned to a strong, robust man, a hunter who knew how to hunt hares, named Perdigat. An incorrigible carouser, a glutton for good food, and little given to overtime, he had the morals of a poacher.

Noting that the aged spouse's health was declining as the lady miller's stomach was growing rounder, Perdigat decided to place the husband in quarantine to protect her. He took a wheelbarrow, put the old man in it, and stashed him in a cabin not far from the mill.

Meunier, tu dors	*Miller, you are sleeping*
Ton moulin va trop vite	*Your mill spins too quickly*
Meunier, tu dors	*Miller, you are sleeping*
Ton moulin va trop fort	*Your mill spins too strong*

When Jeanneton arrived at the mill, he found the place in an advanced state of disrepair, but most importantly his stepmother and Perdigat grunting in the father's sickbed. This rekindled his anger and rage. He foamed at the mouth, and his hands started to tremble.

During the night, by candlelight, Jeanneton searched the mill but did not find his father. After a few hours, he thought of the old shed where broken tools were stored. Feverish and at death's door, the old man was delirious in the foul air, the cold gnawing at his bones. Jeanneton understood that these were his final hours, and he held his hand until the end. The old man told bawdy jokes until his last breath. In the shed, Jeanneton spotted a scythe with a curved, rusted blade; he took it and went back to the mill, transporting the body in the wheelbarrow.

Jeanneton went straight to the marital bedroom. He grabbed his old father's warm body and threw it on the bed where his stepmother and Perdigat lay. When Perdigat – his head still in a fog of grain alcohol – noticed the dead man, he got up to run away, but he tripped and fell. Jeanneton rushed at him to crush his chest under his military boot, calling him a murderer, then grabbed the scythe and, in one swoop, split his skull, killing him outright. Tangled up in her tulle petticoats, Pimparela got up to protest. She slipped in Perdigat's blood, fell on her knees in front of Jeanneton, and begged his forgiveness. He took her firmly in hand and brought her back to the bed, to force her to kiss his father's corpse before knocking her out with the handle of the scythe.

Jeanneton bound the bodies of Pimparela and his father together with rope, like a bundle of sticks. 'For better or for worse,' he spat as he extinguished the lantern and closed the door.

He walked out of the mill, threw the key in the mill basin, and left Noirax.

When the villagers showed up at the mill with their sacks of grain to mill, they were surprised not to hear the reassuring *tic tac* of the millstone. They banged on the door as loudly as they could, in vain. Neighbours came running and decided to knock down the door.

In the room, first they noticed at the foot of the bed the body of Perdigat, fallen in a pool of blood. In the marriage bed, two forms together, lying one on top of the other and bound: the lady miller, her haunted face, her messy hair, her eyes staring and lifeless, and the body of the old husband, smelling of carrion. Pimparela was still breathing but had lost her voice and her mind. And the baby was dead in her belly.

The rumour made the rounds of the village in no time. 'Better drowned than unhappily married,' the gossips sniped.

Pimparela lived several more years after these deaths. The mill became a fortress where she lived as a recluse, surviving winters and the hatred of her people. She even stopped hearing the stones that were thrown at the mill. It was said that she could eat dirt, and illnesses wouldn't affect her. As if death had forgotten her, and it was she who was seeking it.

One fine spring day, with the bloom of the first pimparelas, pretty flowers that grow throughout the prairies of the Centre and that anyone can pick and bring home whenever they want, she was found tied to one of the four blades of the Jorle Mill, dead upside down, her skirt hanging down over her head, her thighs offered up for all to see. The story ended the way it began.

Except that no one came to pick the flower between her legs.

As for Jeanneton, he became neither war hero nor repentant monk. After his crime, he walked, walked, and walked some more. He climbed mountain ranges, hid out in the woods of Saud, then went as far as the Arrière-Pays. Following the roads of Ouestan, he got well past Finistax. He crossed the county limits and continued to walk in the forest, drinking from streams and springs, trapping hare and fishing trout with his bare hands.

After years of wandering, he arrived at the massive doors of a monastery. He confessed having committed a murder of vengeance in a little village in the Centre to defend his father's honour and condemn his stepmother's adultery. He did penance, asked for absolution, and was hired to scrub the rinds of the wheels of Tomme, tend to the monks' garden, and keep the monastery clean. Jeanneton lived a life of poverty and obedience. He died chaste at the age of forty-six, of an affliction of the lungs. Toward the end of his life, sometimes a day would pass that he wouldn't think back to his crime.

He remains to this day the only one who didn't pick the flower.

இ

On the father's land, the horn tree has started to creep. Like the vine, it winds its way under the roots of other groves and always finds its path to the light. It stabs its sole claw into the moist earth, then stands up straight its whole length, invasive and headstrong.

The truth is that nothing can be obtained from this weed, not even Troussepinette or a base to boil spirits. The horn tree soothes no ills and does not intoxicate. It makes you sick like the insidious death cap and the *Boletus satanas*. Its acrid taste is poison and makes the jennies colicky.

No decoction, tincture, or herbal tea can be boiled from the horn tree, no eau de vie, even less a delicate absinthe. The oil of fennel and anise, the milk that tastes like a sort of catechu known as blanquette, collected at the end of distillation to make the next batch, no one will ever obtain it by distilling the horn tree. Aliénor says all sorts of nonsense to the father, who takes her at her word while the weed invades his land. He has the naïveté of the good *King Dagobert, who had his breeches inside out and was hunting the Antwerp plain.*

Le grand saint Éloi	*Great Saint Éloi*
Lui dit: Ô mon roi!	*Says to him: Oh, my king!*
Votre Majesté	*Your Majesty*
Est bien essoufflée	*Is out of breath*
C'est vrai, lui dit le roi	*That's true, says the king*
Un lapin courait après moi	*A rabbit was chasing me*

A new reign has begun.

There was the Era of the Horn and the highly prized milk of the buffalo.

The Era of the Wing, presided over by the Passenger Pigeon Father.

The Era of the Sheep and lambing followed.

All this leads to an idle gentleman, who introduced a few jennies to the estate, fed on hare, pheasant that has been hung, and the odd political ambition.

Every one of them surrendered to the object of his desire. Only one of them failed to protect the land he inherited. That dullard frittered away the family fortune, while people stole it out from his under his nose.

Le grand saint Éloi	*Great Saint Éloi*
Lui dit: Ô mon roi!	*Says to him: Oh, my king!*
Laissez aux oisons	*Let the goslings*
Faire des chansons	*Sing their songs*

Like the creeping plants, thistles, and pimparelas, three species that never grow in monastic gardens, the desideratas' descendants mushroomed. An alliance will soon be formalized between them, and the spell will be cast.

℘

Aliénor goes to the fountain under the eye of the wet nurse, who watches from the window of Malmaison with the tenderness of a mother. The young woman has come to Noirax as a pathfinder, to rework the climax of the story, dictate the missing chapters.

As she leans before the goddess to kiss her marble foot, a drop of pink milk rises to the harridan's breast. Milk and blood combined makes them powerful. The union of desideratas, living and dead, is sealed. In the kingdom of Noirax, the pieces of the puzzle fall into place.

Curtain. Lights.

Intermission.

IV

BENEATH THE WING

HE LOSES BLOOD

xit the green cardboard set, the rolls of artificial grass. Sections of frosted wall have been hung, and white carpet has been unfurled on the ground, sprinkled with plastic flakes that sparkle under the lights.

During the night, heavy, sticky snow has cloaked the landscape and smoothed out its angles. The first blanket of snow landed on the leaves that remained on the branches, making them look like candied mint leaves, like the ones the harridan sometimes uses to decorate pastries and make them pretty. From the estate's antique chimney rises grey smoke that hurls itself into the Noirax sky like a condemned man off a precipice, like a damsel into the jaws of the wolf.

In the forest, under the thick carpet of immaculate velvet, are buried the roots of holy herbs, carcasses of donkeys, the body of a woman, and a secret never told. The father advances along the road that leads to Malmaison wearing a beaver coat and a rabbit muff.

The cep vendor does not visit the estate during the off season, neither does the renderer; they both reappear in the spring, along with the buds, the first mushrooms, and the births of foals. Frost has formed on the marble of the fountain. A small mound of snow has settled on the head and shoulders of the sculpted goddess, and in the hollow of her hip. The knotty branches of the sycamores continue to climb toward *He who observes us from on high, his sights trained on us until our last moment, never relaxing his watch.*

Squeezed flank to flank, the ruminating jennies' breath warms the small farmhouse where they take shelter from the cold.

At the manor, it is dark even at midday, and eyes take a few minutes to adjust to the gloom. An oblique light shines on the father as if through the rose window of a cathedral, striking the blade of a knife planted like a dagger in the acacia wood. In the dining room, the chandelier casts its light on a table full of promise.

With the rigours of winter, we enter into another type of abundance. At the centre of the table, on the beautiful, cracked kaolin plate, a benevolent hand has placed a perfectly roasted capon. In a bowl there are clementines, two pomegranates, a half-peeled lemon and, right beside it, a dish filled with nuts and dried fruit, prunes, figs, and apricots that look like the balls of the castrated donkey whose fatty offal lies in a small porcelain dish that comes from somewhere beyond the Hauts-Pays. A sweet tooth can be satisfied by the mint jelly, pear butter, and groundcherry caramel, to be spread on a fluffy country loaf with a crispy crust that begs to be broken. The fall was generous in pumpkins, winter squash, and calabash; there is every variety and every colour. It is as if the artist Poedras had a bit of fun, one evening of excessive libations, decorating the squash. In a rustic pottery dish lies a row of herring, fished from the Mer Basse. The perfectly aligned little fish, the contrast between the shimmering blue of their scales and the rust of the terracotta, are pleasing to the eye. A mug of steaming tea, a few bottles of red wine, and the delicate breast of a hung partridge complete the table.

The father salivates for a moment before the meal, then turns to the hearth, where the logs are crackling. The fire needs to be fed in this winter that is in a hurry to bury the living. He shifts the logs using an iron poker with a twist pattern (a gift from the black-smith to the Goose Mother to stoke the fire between them), then presses his fur sleeve to his cheek. The softness of the caress makes the blood flow to his sex.

Wearing a hat that belonged to her mother, Jeantylle ventures cautiously down the large staircase. A green satin bow is tied around her tight ringlets drawn up in a small bun behind her head. She has a hoop in one ear and has lined her eyelids with kohl. Pampelune's short purple boots with black beading are constricting her ankles, but you must suffer to be beautiful, she is told.

'From now on, I will be Jeantylle!'

This is the first time she has appeared to her loved ones.

'Beautiful! Utterly superb!' Aliénor exclaims as she watches her gripping the handrail to avoid collapsing because of the boots squeezing her feet.

The father and the harridan are speechless. It's rare that the father has nothing to say. To fill the silence and relax the atmosphere, Aliénor starts to hum the first tune that comes to mind:

Dansons la capucine	*Let's dance the nasturtium*
Y a pas de pain chez nous	*There is no bread at home*
Y en a chez la voisine	*There is at our neighbour's*
Mais ce n'est pas pour nous	*But it is not for us*

The contrast between the opulence of the menu, the heat of the fire in the hearth, the Crémant chilling in the bucket of snow, and an old song about the penniless is painfully ironic. The father fiddles with the tip of his moustache, and the harridan fingers the set of keys in her apron pocket, as if to assure herself that they are all there.

With her falsetto voice, which approaches a female contralto, Jeantylle takes up the song:

On pleure chez la voisine   *They cry at our neighbour's*
On rit toujours chez nous   *We always laugh at home.*
Youh!   *Whoop!*

Aliénor joins her at the foot of the stairs and holds out her hand to invite her to dance. After a moment of hesitation, the harridan joins them. As tradition would have it, the three women join hands in a circle and crouch down on the 'Whoop!'

'Take off your boots. It will be easier!' Aliénor suggests.

Jeantylle complies and starts dancing again, until the smell of male sweat scents her shaved armpits. Little by little, she is going to learn self-awareness, the manifestations of the physical body that must be suppressed and camouflaged as a woman, because all the magic and mystery in the world depend on the dissimulation.

The father silently knocks back his glass as he watches them dance.

After the dance, they go back to the table. The father fills the flutes with what remains of the Crémant. It will take a lot of alcohol to wash all this down.

'When will we be able to drink Aliénor's absinthe?' Jeantylle asks, as she takes a pickled herring from the plate.

'In the spring. Once the crown of the wormwood and the horn of the tree have broken through the humus, I will be able to boil a first batch of spirits.'

Content with the answer, the father tears open the bread, while the harridan grabs a knife to carve the capon. Jeantylle cracks the shell of a hazelnut and bites into it. Aliénor opens the jar of mint jelly, spreads it on the warm bread, wolfs it all down, slurping. She barks that it is exquisite.

'Pampelune loved mint jelly,' the father says, drifting away on a memory.

Her mouth full, in an almost casual tone, Aliénor takes this small opening as a chance to ask the question that nags at her.

'What happened to Pampelune, anyway?'

The harridan drops a drumstick on the plate set out for the bones. At the bottom of the bowl, in the blue porcelain, a man in a wig and frock coat pushes a merry woman of easy virtue on a swing, as she exposes her ankle to him.

Once upon a time there was a story that can't be told, the words of which crossed no lips: the story of the desideratas, written in white ink.

It is the story of life lurking in the shadows, in the margins and the night, healthy and thriving. A story that is older than the world itself, the tale of those who must kill to survive. Perhaps it would be better to turn it into a song and set it to a cheery chorus.

It all started with a little girl abandoned in the woods when the wolf wasn't there. She was taken in by a trapper, clothed in skins and fur, fed bear meat that tasted of iron. That would make a pretty verse, the beginning of a song with woodsy charm.

The latest news is that the perfume has turned, a donkey is dead, the rotor of the Jorle Mill is as still as the hands of the grandfather clock, the house will collapse onto the memories and the smell of fear. It is a story that is written in snow, with milk and sperm. It cannot be told, but it can be sung. Or made into a fragrance.

The father sighs loudly and appears suddenly weary.

'I will tell you about it another time. When it is dark.'

Aliénor buries her hand in the body of the capon and pulls on the bird's shoulder girdle.

'While we wait, let's snap the wishbone!'

The harridan is at the window looking toward the forest. Her breath is shallow, waiting for someone who doesn't appear or for the truth to explode. In the deep pocket of her servant's apron, she fingers the four keys, those to the Berthoumieux manors, shed, and cellar. The harridan looks like she is hiding a secret.

The bone cracks, and Aliénor gets to make a wish.

'May fools become kings! May flowers become fruit! May the dead be resurrected! May the light shine on what has remained in the shadows!'

She laughs heartily, but what flows from the eruption is not joy – maybe fury? She laughs a forced laugh that rings hollow, the way others spit, pinch, and bite. She laughs as if something were itching her, and this laugh foretells a minor revolution.

'May the beggars become kings like at Carnival!' Aliénor continues, in an almost sadistic spirit. 'May Sesame open! May the day arrive!'

The father feels his wound throb and holds back tears. The words have been growing in his flesh for a few months, and the gash will not close. He has lost weight; the pain leaves less room for appetite. He drinks to numb it, swallows his third glass in one gulp, but the alcohol works only for a moment to dull the feeling of the words escaping through his wound. The father takes leave of his loved ones and goes up to his room. As soon as he removes his shirt, a swarm of little curled papers unfurls down to the ground. Like streamers at a children's birthday party. He wants to read them, but when he pulls on one, the pain is so sharp that it is as if his skin is being torn. He takes a deep breath, grabs the end of the strip, tears it off, and almost faints. The father pulls himself together and reads: 'No one should walk through that door.' The harridan had warned him.

He searches for a song to hum to take his mind off things, to give him some courage, but no tune comes to him. He is no longer the hero of the story. He has had his turn. He went looking for a fall, charged headlong into it, and now the story is being written on him. The moment has come when the protagonists have to yield place and privilege to the supporting characters.

♡

With Aliénor's arrival in Noirax, as he spent time with her, Jeanty, who was already tempted to give his desires free rein and reveal his true nature, mustered the courage to take off his man's casing and embrace the woman inside him. Jeantylle had never met anyone so dangerous and true. This throbbing, blustering, probing, scrutinizing presence has triggered a metamorphosis. In the forest, in the buildings, in the harridan, and in the father's flesh, something is unfolding and will be revealed.

Jeantylle does not deny it: she likes young ladies and soldiers. With the heart and soul of a desiderata, she awaits the return of Malbrough. Advancing through the world, arms open like this, makes her want to dance, to celebrate, to kiss. Why choose and limit yourself if you desire both tank driver and hazelnut vendor?

Appearances can be deceiving. Those who are well-born are not who we think they are. Beggars are not so destitute. In the bird there was a fledgling. When sung to the final verse, children's songs turn into dark poems or sadistic tales. Fortunes can go up in smoke, manors crumble, fires go out, and the world order can be turned on its head.

Au clair de la lune	*In the light of the moon*
On n'y voit qu'un peu	*Not much can be seen*
On chercha la plume	*We looked for the quill*
On chercha le feu	*We looked for the fire*
En cherchant d'la sorte	*Searching like this*
Je n'sais c'qu'on trouva	*I don't know what was found*
Mais j'sais que la porte	*But I do know that the door*
Sur eux se ferma	*Closed on them*

ം

'Try to remember how it happened,' the doctor again suggests, as he cleans the father's wounds.

'There was llama, a hot-air balloon, bad wine … and an iridescent dress. The party in the village was in full swing. It's as if in the forest I was … marked. As if the forest marked me.'

The doctor and the harridan exchange looks, seeming to signify that this man is being a drama queen, and they are running out of patience.

'Marked … by the branches of a tree?'

'No. By a large animal. A horned animal.'

The father closes his eyes and plays back the beginning of the scene to himself.

It's summer, the green set returns. He is on the dirt road that goes to the presbytery, being led by Aliénor into the forest. The buzz of fireflies, a psychedelic dress, the seams of which are showing. Ferns, young deciduous trees, nocturnal birds, it is as if nature bows as she passes. She floats, this woman who is leading him on a walk and who has not yet surrendered, like an apple in his hand for him to bite into. She holds out a magic mushroom to him. 'Try this,' she commands, 'and chew it slowly before swallowing.'

He loses sight of her for a moment but keeps advancing through the dark. Soon she stops answering. The father takes off his shoes because the wet ground is sucking him down as he steps, swallowing and erasing his tracks. To warn the animals of his presence, he sings the first song that comes to mind.

Ne pleure pas, Jeannette	*Don't cry, Jeannette*
Nous te marierons	*We will marry you off*
Avec le fils d'un prince	*To the son of a prince*
Alazim boum boum	*Alazim boom boom*
Alazim boum boum	*Alazim boom boom*
Avec le fils d'un prince	*To the son of a prince*
Ou celui d'un baron	*Or the son of a baron*

Aliénor also takes off her high-heeled boots and sings the next lines:

Je ne veux pas d'un prince	*I don't want a prince*
Alazim boum boum	*Alazim boom boom*
Alazim boum boum	*Alazim boom boom*
Je ne veux pas d'un prince	*I don't want a prince*
Encore moins d'un baron	*Even less a baron*

Oh! Aliénor's pretty little boot! Its narrowness stirs something in the father, and he smiles and takes up the song:

Je veux mon ami Pierre	*I want my dear Pierre*
Alazim boum boum	*Alazim boom boom*
Alazim boum boum	*Alazim boom boom*
Je veux mon ami Pierre	*I want my dear Pierre*
Celui qu'est en prison	*The one who is in prison*

She knows the words. She wants to play and sing with him. *You won't have your Pierre, alazim boom boom, alazim boom boom.* The father advances toward the husky voice, magnetic north, and discovers, dropped on the path, Aliénor's phlox crown, the one that makes her look like a queen.

Tu n'auras pas ton Pierre	*You won't have your Pierre*
Nous le pendouillerons	*We will hang him*

If you hang Pierre, hang me with him, she goes on, taking off her garter belt.

Then Aliénor starts to unlace the tight corset of the dress.

And we hanged Peter, and his Jeannette along with him! How lovely it is to sing in call and response from one end of the grove to the other, the father thinks, just before slipping on a bit of fabric and twisting his ankle, ending up lying stretched out on the iridescent dress. Baroque music, a broken promise, a rainbow, then the vision of a woman burning him with a torch – is it a premonition? The sublime gives way to the ridiculous. The small stage on which he held the floor and everyone's attention, and the man soon to be mayor, seem so far away. On all fours in the muck, he tries to get back on his feet, but his twisted ankle is causing him pain.

He hears a body dive into the pond. Good idea, the cold water will help. The father undresses too. 'Yoo-hoo!' She is calling to him; it's a game!

A game of hunting, in which the roles have just been reversed.

The rustle of wings, a sound of rubber slapping. Four bats take flight in front of the father. 'What are you waiting for? Are you coming?' She is promising him a festival of the senses, a forbidden romance. 'Hurry!'

Hobbling awkwardly toward this honeyed voice that calls out to him – like grenadine – he trips on the knotted root of an oak tree and catches himself from falling at the last minute, but his ankle is throbbing terribly.

'You're taking too long! I'm getting tired of waiting,' the voice warns.

It is as though the origin of it has shifted. The father turns around, careful not to stumble a second time. More bats! They brush the small crown of skin at the top of his head, where hair no longer grows. The father panics, one hand on his head, the other hiding his sex.

'I'm leaving,' Aliénor says.

'No! Wait!'

And that's when he spots, still and looming, the shadow of a large horned animal. The father whistles through his teeth to scare off the creature. The animal, in the prime of its life, raises an imposing rack of antlers in all its glory. It turns its head in the father's direction and takes a moment to consider the injured prey looking pathetic before it. The predator detects the heady aroma of fear, which excites it. It advances in the dark, moving through a thick silence.

The father whistles again and spits like a cat, which seems to provoke the animal. So he changes his strategy and tries to appear less combative. The father turns his back to the large animal and beats a retreat, making his way painfully through the mire. The creature charges him, antlers first, and suddenly the father is enveloped in the large animal's shadow.

The antlers are thrust into him twice. The father rolls in the ditch on the side of the road and plays dead, while the animal moves on toward something more euphoria inducing, a piercing call in the night, a big burst of laughter. The father was merely an obstacle in its path.

Abandoned in the ditch, stark naked and shivering, the father no longer has the heart to sing. There are two long, painful welts on his back, not to mention his swollen ankle and his heel turning blue. The air enters his flesh, the ground mixes in with it. In the distance he hears the furious gallop of a roaring beast and the giggle of a woman who is riding it.

❧

While, in the bedroom, the story of the desideratas is being written on the father's back, Aliénor gingerly advances barefoot through the snow, balancing on the cold as if on a beach of burning sand. She is humming, to bring a bit of joy and levity back to her heart, to create a diversion as she heads toward the house that makes her nervous, where she doesn't like to live. *Open your door to me, for the love of God.*

In the Perfume House, the windows are steamed up as if someone has just taken a hot bath. A melody can be heard in the distance, a darker song than it would seem at first. Black with a tinge of blue. The voice of a man lets itself be overtaken by that of a woman, lower and earthier. It's beautiful. Like a funeral dance or an innocent poem that suggests that this world could be smooth as satin. But the word *temperate* falls near the word *tempest* in the dictionary. One slips so easily into the other, and this condensation on the windows is a layer of grime that will have to be cleaned to clearly see the memories that weigh down the house.

As she turns the delicate oval doorknob to open the perfume cabinet, Aliénor's hand trembles. 'No one should walk through that door,' the harridan had repeated ... But which one? The door to the manor, the perfume cabinet, the door of the song, of Malmaison, or the doors to the city? Why shouldn't they? In whose interest would ignorance be best?

The melody swells until it fills the space. The man and the woman have stopped singing, and now someone is playing the piano. The music is perfect and full. Each chord calls to the next. It is easier to compose a melody than to rewrite history. In front of the piano, one simply needs to touch the black keys and then return to the white. The resulting melancholy is soothing. No need to add words, to plaster lyrics on top, to force a rhyme: the melody is enough.

The cabinet door hasn't been opened in a long time. The door-knob turns with a subtle crack, the sound of a goose egg breaking.

On the walnut shelves, there are a dozen blown-glass vials, all different, lined up like rare books in a library, each one with a title, a memory, and a story. Aliénor pulls the stopper from the first vial, and a blond child springs into the light. The mother is a small, frail woman with bloodshot eyes who has just expelled life from her belly, with all the strength that she had and then some. Now she wants to sleep, but she can't, because a life depends on her own. No one is watching over her anymore, and her days are numbered. This perfume is called *Dawn's First Light*, and Pampelune has diluted bergamot, lemon from Saud, and a bit of iridescent raspberry to create an accord that exudes the joy, hope, and mystery of a new destiny.

Aliénor opens the second vial, and the top note is ginger, which prickles the nostrils before emitting an accord of blood and stale tobacco. Wafts of sandalwood and leather appear. The name of this perfume is *Hunting with Hounds*, and the flat voice of a female cousin breaks through, resigned to the violence. They claimed that by mistake the hunting dogs had been released too early, before the bugle sounded. Twenty-two years old, pregnant. Dead, devoured right down to the womb by famished dogs. What was she doing running alone through the forest, breathless? The desideratas often died suddenly, because their destiny was tragedy, people said. They unsaddled the purebreds, put away the bugle, and the hunt did not take place. Or, rather, it had already taken place.

The next perfume is *Eau de Protection*. Extract of devilwood and jasmine absolute, essence of styrax, honey, and chili. Pampelune must have worn it all the time. A perfume that squeezes the heart and compresses the chest, because it hides the truth as protection.

The gentle aroma of regret hidden under a corset, and a warning: 'Trust no one!'

The music stops; Aliénor deciphers the memories hidden in the perfumes with even greater acuity. With the haste of someone who wants to know and understand, she pulls the stoppers from all the vials and gains access to the missing chapters of a woman's life. *Milky Mint* tells the story of Jeanty's childhood, *Male Species* spreads its musk and a strange essence of resinoid. *Winter on the Estate*, with its notes of iris and ambergris, tells of the boredom of the long months of a season spent waiting as if in the belly of a whale.

The story is cryptic; Aliénor cannot grasp all of its subtleties, particularly since some of the perfumes have turned. She wants to wear only one of Pampelune's creations: *Suddenly, a Deer*, homage to the loam of the Centre with pine, laurel, lily of the valley, rose de mai, and a milky note of tuberose. She tips a few drops on her wrists, then presses them to the backs of her ears and her knees. Careful! *Suddenly, a Deer* awakens the mistrust needed for survival and exudes a disquieting accord. Reminiscence of animals born, raised, hunted, and killed on this land. Night rounds, surveillance, predation, capture. Weapons born in the fire of the forge to punish lovers by eliminating those who disobey. A messy order that must be rejected and overthrown.

The last perfume she smells is called *The Truth*. Two words, eight narrow blue letters. There is no liquid inside; how odd. The truth has no smell? Was Pampelune working on this perfume when her life was cut short? The glass vial slips from Aliénor's hands and shatters on the ground. Dusk descends suddenly like a guillotine.

Pampelune, alone in the forest, surrounded by the sounds she is making: her breath, her feet slapping on the ground, her heart hammering against her chest in dull thuds.

She is running, barefoot, taking care not to trip. She is like Snow White on the lam, with no kindly doe to come to her aid. There is only her swift pace. A gunshot, she jumps. The hunt begins, and the acrid smell of fear is released as the top note.

She hasn't run like this in a long time. The last time, Pampelune was a child and wanted to get to the top of a hill fast to take in the view over the Mer Basse. From the other side of the pond a voice rises up in an echo that tells her there is only one place to hide in the forest: the Berthoumieuxs' cellar. 'There is no point in resisting. Stay there, panicked but calm. Locate worry between the two extremes and hang on until the end.' The echo is a warning, but its advice protects no one.

The moon is a silken thread, the reflection of which drowns in the pond while Pampelune catches her breath. Hiding in the only place possible, the charnel house, is all there is left to do. She doesn't have the key, but the unlocked door easily gives way.

The heart note is clammy, trembling, and cold: the odour of the night rises over the smell of fear.

Et viennent les pas nus	*So come the naked footsteps*
Un à un	*One by one*
Comme les premières gouttes de pluie	*Like the first drops of rain*
Au fond du puits	*At the bottom of the well*

The cold numbs Pampelune's memories and paralyzes her gestures. As she descends, the desires, passions, and inner storms lull. The blaze weakens, and the dark rises up. Here, in total darkness, rest is finally possible. With the immobility of the body, the mouth can still sing, and thoughts can still circulate. The echo whispers that there is no point in trying to warm up; the moment will be needlessly prolonged. 'Turn your head, watch the fathers sleeping so tranquilly, and see how they are at peace.' Pampelune *gazes with astonishment*

À même les noirs ossements	*As set on the black bones*
Luire les pierres bleues incrustées	*Shine the blue encrusted stones*

Once, when she was a little towheaded girl, she got lost in the woods chasing a butterfly. Alone in the middle of the forest, she sang the 'Litanie du Feu' – the 'Litany of the Fire' – at the top of her lungs so someone would find her. For the fire to warm you, you have to sing its praises, herald its heat, light, goodwill, and effort, and celebrate its beauty. *Hurray for the fire's embers, hurray for its embers!* The plan worked; she was found, her face smeared with soil, the tips of her fingers numb from the cold, dishevelled, belting out:

Feu, feu, joli feu	*Fire, fire, lovely fire*
Ton ardeur nous réjouit	*Your blaze is a delight*
Feu, feu, joli feu	*Fire, fire, lovely fire*
Monte dans la nuit	*Rise up in the night*

She should have stayed in the forest, rather than going to hide in the cellar. Now she is almost dead, searching for daylight, like a poor little bird in the mine. The echo has followed her and keeps talking with the malevolent calm of an opioid. 'Try to sleep; it shouldn't be hard. Orpheus has abandoned you, but Morpheus awaits. Go on, release your breath, atone. Your profile will be forever young in the cameo and on the funeral bookmark, and that is what is expected of you. Now die. Complete your death to interrupt your bloodline, and let someone else move ahead.'

The base note of the perfume is sulphurous. It is the note of a flame, of burning, of cremation. There is danger, but it's too late. The fire conquers fear and the night, and gives one the desire to dance, to start to live loudly again, to abandon oneself to the music. In the crypt, lying next to the fathers, Pampelune starts singing with a wisp of a voice and a few remaining snippets of hope the 'Litany of the Fire.' *Hurray for the song of the fire, hurray for its song!* But her voice falls silent before the next chorus.

Cue the storybook narrator: *You are dead now, you'll never know. Dead in the cellar, of fear, a shadow in a nightgown. Who locked you away? Was it her, while feeding your son, who almost became her own? Are bonds of milk stronger than bonds of blood? It isn't your fault that you found yourself on the bright side, in the golden light and the right house. But you are the one who was sacrificed, Pampelune. You lost a fight that has been waged since long before the two of you. You shouldn't have trusted anyone. You believed you were wellborn, but that doesn't mean anything anymore. Here lies a fool who died of her own innocence. They will erect the most sumptuous of tombs, set with the remaining fragments of kaolin. Your bones will be buried in the ground under a headstone where wild garlic, lily of the valley, and a clump of pimparelas will grow.*

Aliénor tries to snatch from the air a last whiff of the perfume, a few traces of the story, and that is when she spots a tiny hand stretched out toward her. When she opens her eyes, there are only the shards of glass from the broken vial and questions that remain unanswered.

ustling tissue paper and the deafening crepitation of male cicadas in the middle of a punishing summer. A butterfly escapes from the open palms of a young Jeanty, who is singing in a small androgynous voice:

Ah! vous dirai-je, maman	*Oh! Mommy, shall I tell you*
Ce qui cause mon tourment	*What is tormenting me*

Kneeling near him, Pampelune was picking herbs for her perfumes.

'Some flowers release their most majestic aromas when you cut their stem, then they fade entirely, as if going out with a bang, so they are not forgotten. They are ostentatious and ephemeral, and not meant for perfumery,' she observed.

'How I would like to have a nose like yours!' Jeanty said in admiration.

'You inherited the aquiline nose of the fathers, which makes you look like an eaglet.'

'I mean a nose like yours to be able to read secrets in bouquets of flowers.'

'Come closer. I want to show you something.'

Looking toward Malmaison to make sure no one was watching, she said, lowering her voice: 'Breathe in here, near my ribs, and you will discover the smell of fear.'

Jeanty had already detected this smell on his mother but that day it was much more acrid than usual.

'I would like to wear dresses, too.'

Pampelune seemed surprised.

'When we are alone in the house. But don't ever tell your father. Come on, let's go in now. It's time for your piano lesson.'

The little prince was learning to play *Oh! Mommy, shall I tell you.*

In the Era of the Sheep, on the Berthoumieux estate, the father had learned to kill animals while caressing their necks, the right way in the right place, such that sheep, paralyzed from the sense of well-being, grew weak and fell to their knees. 'Don't resist,' the father would whisper, 'death will come anyway.' And, when the little ram buckled, the knife slit its throat and the blood sprayed. Pain and pleasure united in the pink wool and the final exhalation.

Then came Héléna, the fountain goddess, the Sheep Father's drowned desiderata. In the early morning, she was found floating in the water of the basin, hair fanned out, dead. In the same position as Pampelune, lifeless in the cellar, poisoned, hair fanned out, dead. Before dying, Héléna had time to give birth to a child and send her off into the woods.

Many other goddesses lived in the shadows in the small buildings on the estate. The nubile grace of the concubines versus the rights of the wives is at the origin of a prolific line of half-siblings.

Rumours are circulating in the village that the Berthoumieux family is in decline, that the Perfume House will collapse and the land will revolt. But desire always triumphs, even once the fire is out.

Aliénor has the robustness and the purple hair of the harridan, the determination of a buffalo; Jeantylle has the sensitivity of

Pampelune and her golden curls. As the son and his privilege fade, the half-siblings grow closer.

The bond of the harridan's nourishing milk meets the bond of the wife's blood. This pink cream, soluble in the father's blood, has irrigated the Berthoumieux land, causing a family tree to take root with branches that resemble the frenetic advance of a rare disease.

How many infants have been abandoned in the woods? How many survived? How many danced with wolves? How many produced descendants?

The heirs are recognizable with their greenish skin, their thick hair, their purple patch of down. They know how to write and know their rights. They arrive with the strength of numbers. Wearing steel-toed boots to walk the fatherland, they have nothing to lose and everything to gain. They know they are bonded by milk, as well as by blood. The time has come to lift the axe high, to take a run-up and chop the branch. The branch is no longer on the tree, the tree has lost its leaves. This line is dying. The song is done.

As for the father, he keeps piling the many unread letters in a lovely transparent box. He will hand them over to the notary soon, he claims, deep in denial. The supreme irony is that the little antique box has a golden lock embossed with a B for Berthoumieux, just like the one that adorns the door to the cellar – a creation of the lady blacksmith, the one who hammered the metal as she burned with desire for the Goose Mother. There are so many letters piled up in the box that the lid no longer shuts. The father stopped staring at the forest when his aspiring politician's eye turned toward the village. This is why he doesn't see them, closing in, rage in their hearts and hearts on their fists, crawling through the forest of Noirax, which is never the accomplice one thinks. From inside the manor, when you look toward the forest, you can see, even at night, azure eyes looking back toward Malmaison.

The illegitimate daughters, united in semi-sorority, were the ones who put Aliénor on the father's trail. Even leaving from Saud, she arrived in the Centre region before them, knife between her teeth, rage in her heart, moved by the desire to topple the privilege. Aliénor, the pathfinder, canary in the mine, and collector of memories. She no longer has the heart to sing. In her head, questions swirl and collide.

Who decides the goings-on in children's songs and nursery rhymes? For instance, why hang Pierre and Jeannette?

Why did Jack jump over a candlestick?

Why couldn't the old man get up in the morning?

Why couldn't all the king's horses and all the king's men put Humpty Dumpty back together again?

Who is this all-powerful storyteller, who never questions their decisions, who constantly makes bad choices?

Why does the lassie go this way and that way?

Where, oh where has my little dog gone?

Who baked the blackbirds in a pie? Why cut off the mice's tails with a carving knife? Why does baby come down, cradle and all? Why did the spider sit down beside her? Why do (husha husha) we all fall down?

Why kiss the girls and make them cry?

Who killed Cock Robin?

Who murdered Pampelune?

☙

Lined up on the vanity are powders, shadows, concealer, kohl pencils to create a beauty mark, a pointy brush to outline doe eyes.

In front of the mirror, Jeantylle notices that the stubble under the makeup is growing in with a little less vigour than before she started drinking the lichen infusions. Her chin has grown more delicate, her odour has softened; from some angles she is the woman she has always wanted to be. She pulls on the corset laces of Aliénor's fanciful dress. 'Here, I want you to have it. You want it more than me.' The light, flattering fabric slides over her skin and excites her. It feels so nice to be in silk, to be oneself.

Her hand in Aliénor's, they will go together *to where love is fragrant, to remake their nest. They will go to where the day dies. Somewhere else is too far*, so it will be here, close by.

In an oval pine frame, there is the famous painting by Poedras, *Mother and Child*, a son snuggled like a lamb in the arms of his mother. Pampelune has returned to Malmaison. Jeantylle recognizes her smell. And the grandfather clock is keeping time again.

Something has resumed.

എ

In the shed, at the end of the garden, a woman is writing furiously enough to rupture her shoulder blade. She will be at it a while; she needs to rewrite history, strike while the iron is hot so that the truth resurfaces and flows like a bottleneck filled with cream.

Sentences slip from the tale and imprint themselves on the father's back. The words line up like warnings or riddles. The father's son is going hunting with his beautiful silver gun. Snippets of seemingly innocent songs, riddles, and rhymes that make him suspicious, incidentally drop crumbs of truth. *Let's go walk in the woods, while the father isn't here.* Holes are being bored in the secrets to give them some air. *Here comes the good wind, here comes the nice wind.*

The party is over. The father will hunt no more, or sing, or strut.

The chorus of voices will rise up without his tenor, with the warning that from beneath his wing he is losing his station and blood, that *diamonds are coming out of his eyes and gold and silver out of his beak.*

Toutes ses plumes s'en vont au vent
Trois dames s'en vont les ramassant

His feathers are flying off in the wind
Three women are collecting them

V

SHEEP'S WOOL

ust like a thousand other times since Pampelune's death, Jeantylle's fingertips caress the kaolin fragments set in the gravestone. She never wanted to start up the Jorle Mill, to make the rotor turn again. That was her father's idea, not hers. Since putting Aliénor's magic dress back on – the one with the seams showing – she has had many other desires.

With the material stored in the attic, exquisite fabrics from distant lands, she spends her days designing and sewing dresses. Aliénor is her model, taking delight in trying on all her creations, happily wrapping the fabric around her and parading through the forest before the small society of flowers.

The father, who is wasting away, almost never leaves his bedroom. Twice a week, the mustachioed good doctor comes to examine his wounds, still open and even more gaping. The doctor leaves Malmaison each time looking stunned. The father smokes and pops everything science has to offer – and more still – to alleviate his pain: opium, morphine, and their derivatives, an extreme pharmacopeia in which any combination is allowed. While he develops addictions to these substances that make him see life in fluorescent colour, members of the household imply that the father is resting to recuperate, that it is best not to bother him right now, blah-blahblah. He will have to shelve his political aspirations and cancel his election campaign. His dreams of being all powerful are aborted. The keys to the city will go to someone else. For the moment, he prefers to live in denial and the company of psychotropic drugs.

Aliénor makes more and more trips to the garden shed with a tray filled with provisions, which is empty when she returns. She is bringing food to the woman in the shed who has started putting a long tale into words, so she can keep writing like a Fury, day and night, bent over her work, with the concentration it requires. The harridan has taken care of others long enough. It's her turn to make her voice heard. The future of the blood heirs depends upon it. She no longer wants to eat meat; her diet consists of fruit, nuts, omelettes, sardines, and bread, and plenty of steaming pots of tea. Sometimes she emerges from the shed, goes to the fountain, and meditates for a while before the marble goddess. Sometimes she ventures as far as Pampelune's grave, kneels, and murmurs something that resembles a prayer but is not.

In addition to the writer, Aliénor watches over the three jennies and the colt that is almost a yearling. The month of March is particularly mild; she sends them off to toss their heads in the pasture, monitors the growth of wolf teeth in the mouth of the little donkey and sings with the spirit of a governess, going off-key when the note rises.

Dent de loup	Wolf tooth
Dent de loup	Wolf tooth
Dent de loup, loup, loup	Wolf tooth, tooth, tooth
Loup des bois	Wolf of the woods

Loup des bois	*Wolf of the woods*
Loup des bois, bois, bois	*Wolf of the woods, woods, woods*

The foal has lost almost all its down; a clump remains near the withers. Aliénor massages the dry chestnuts of the jennies with goose fat to soften them. The toes of their hoofs have grown longer in the past few months. The equids need so much care, it's a shame not to be able to ride them. She calls the blacksmith to come trim their feet and file their teeth. She asks him if he wouldn't mind bringing the mail when he comes, because the Berthoumieuxs haven't been to the post office in ages.

Boîte aux lettres	*Mailbox*
Boîte aux lettres	*Mailbox*
Boîte aux lettres, lettres, lettres	*Mailbox, box, box*
Lettre d'amour	*Love letter*
Lettre d'amour	*Love letter*
Lettre d'amour, mour, mour	*Letter love, love, love*

In the shed, the hand slides furiously across the paper. The words soar, the ideas flow and run away with themselves. The period at the end of a sentence becomes a small fire of joy. The writing is gushing and volcanic; the hand struggles to follow the movement of thought that sweeps it along. This woman hadn't given in to her desire in so long. Writing is power, she had almost forgotten. As the story advances, light is shed on the world. She senses as she writes the invisible threads connecting the living, reads the future in the cursive letters, but more importantly the past. She looks over her shoulder, focuses as she looks back at old episodes to revisit the key scenes of the play. It is only the beginning of the story.

At the end of the small century-old bridge, on the lane with the sycamores, their branches imploring *He who observes us from on high, his sights trained on us until our last moment, never relaxing his watch*, an old man appears, cane in hand, and stops from time to time to spit in a handkerchief. A Dalmatian follows him, jumps, pants, bites the fallen branches as it shakes its head, then joins his master when whistled for. Crouched in the thickets, the hares hold their breath to evade the dog's long burrowing snout.

Tracking, predation. It always comes down to that.

The father pulls back the bedroom curtain to watch for the arrival of an old man with a handsome face and long white hair. The last time the painter Poedras set foot on the estate was to paint Pampelune's portrait. Wearing a creation by Jeantylle – a bright green silk dress with an empire waist – Aliénor greets the old man and ushers him into Malmaison.

When he enters, Poedras comes face to face with his painting of the stone manor. He immediately notices the addition of a detail to the canvas, a small hand pulling the purple curtain in the master bedroom closed.

'It looks like a woman's hand, but I can't be sure,' he says, pointing to the painting.

'This painting is full of mystery. The ivy running along the building turning away from the sunlight … That invention was intentional, wasn't it? You were trying to provoke a reaction.'

A smile spreads across the artist's face.

'I was having a bit of fun. I had given up hope of anyone ever noticing! I remember giving this painting a title that appears nowhere but in my head: *Disobedience*. I am delighted that someone dared paint on the canvas. That person is getting dangerously close to the truth, but they need to keep searching ... Searching in another way.'

'It's a treasure hunt?'

'In a way. There is no time limit.'

'What brings you to Malmaison?'

'Two rumours. They say in the village that the father Berthoumieux is unwell and won't recover in time for the election.'

'Indeed, he is wounded and resting.'

'What is the nature of his ailment?'

'A story is being written on his back, against his will, fissuring his skin.'

The hundred-year-old man is silently perplexed, then he bursts out laughing.

'My little lady, you are deliriously entertaining. I would like to hire you as a model.'

'I have better things to do than to play the muse. I am taking care of the donkeys and watching over the woman who is writing. And the second rumour?'

Poedras lowers his voice.

'They say the harridan is back. I would like to speak with her.'

'You will have to wait, because we can't disturb her from her work, except to bring her tea and eggs. While you wait, why don't you get reacquainted with your paintings!'

Outside, the Dalmatian has had time to devour a good half dozen young hares. Its muzzle covered in blood, it tears around barking, tossing up their blue-grey fluff and watching it swirl as if painting an immense canvas in the air.

She comes to the end of the chapter she is writing, satisfied. The muscles in her forearm are numb and her right shoulder blade makes a strange popping sound when she stretches. Time for a break. She grabs the key ring from her apron pocket, locks the door to the shed, and heads to the side of the house. The outdoor shower is behind a low wall, and she goes in. Every time she writes it stokes desire in her. Her hand and the foam slip between her thighs. The same old fantasy with the father Berthoumieux invites itself into her thoughts. The outdated inclinations that linger, flesh offered and then devoured in a dream. She drives away the memory as soon as the passion subsides.

She comes out of the shower and for the first time puts on clothes that Jeantylle designed for her. Puffy, silky, and joyful, an ample outfit in bright colours. No more black dress and maid's hairdo. No more goodness, selflessness, and self-denial. Suddenly she wants a nap.

In Malmaison, the centenarian painter hobbles from canvas to canvas. His paintings, portraits, and charcoal drawings are like memories that emerge abruptly. He refuses any explanation, lingers on certain details, is enraptured by the realism of a fig stem, is moved by the rough rendering of a rope knotted around the paws of a hanging hare, holds back a tear before the contrast between the purple of the plums and the white verging on blue of the porcelain jug of a still life. Before *Fire in an Old Forge*, a painting commissioned by the Goose Mother to represent the burning love between two women, the old man becomes chatty. 'The mother wanted to be able to admire the piece without the Passenger Pigeon Father suspecting anything; that's why the flame is blue, very bright. Look at the heat of that blue!' he says, astonished. 'The same flame burns in your left eye.'

He stops at painting after painting: *Naked Woman at the Fountain, Woolly Sheep, Young Rebel and Lamb, Fresh Almonds in the Shell, Flock of Geese, Abundant Chaos of an English Garden, Rest of the Barnacle Goose* … Almost all of them are realist, with small details that slip the yoke of reality and its edict to be faithful. Making a perfect copy of nature is not an act of the divine, and the keen eye delights in finding irregularities in Poedras's paintings. Like the ugly little duck with cyan plumage, crouched among the sleeping Canada geese, or the dung beetle with the golden shell on the plate of almonds. See the green sky over the goddess, and the pink milk she is pouring from her jug. The young iconoclast is a convent schoolgirl. The ram has just inseminated his mother ewe. The naked woman at the fountain hides a weapon behind her thigh. In the English garden, behind a bunch of pimparelas, a little monkey gropes its genitals and sticks out its tongue. Despite the apparent order of things, everything is askew. You need to learn how to see better, my child.

'Without art, I would be dispossessed of the world. To be able to paint, I hold landscapes, fruit, nuts, animals, and flowers tight in my hand. And you, young lady, what do you possess? What do you have that is precious, hidden in the palm of your hand?'

Aliénor shows him her empty hands.

'Nothing. I have only the rage in my heart.'

'Rage calls for a bright pigment … Would it be … mustard yellow? Or magenta? Rust like oxidized iron. I have never painted nor possessed it.'

'Mine is the colour of mould and suffocation: verdigris.'

'Maybe one day desire will take the place of the rage. Then you will be both queen and subject.'

'I want to move past this and deliver myself from the rage.'

'Can you squeeze it tight in your hand and paint it?'

'No.'

'Then keep searching for its source. You are on the right path, my child.'

'Mr. Poedras ... It's about the mother and child, the ones you painted.'

'The convergence lines will soon cross. And then perspective will replace illusion.'

'I don't understand the nonsense you spout!'

'Papa wants me to reason like a big person; but I say that reason is worth more than dried sausage.'

They come to the large oval painting, the portrait of Pampelune and Jeanty sketched in the light with respectful restraint, as if they were the Virgin and Child. Upon seeing the son curled up in the mother's arms, Poedras feels his heart clench and his knees weaken. Aliénor takes that moment to strike.

'I'm trying to find out what happened to this woman.'

'They say she ran off in the night. They found her tracks in the forest. They needed to point the finger at someone; the Berthou-mieuxs accused the wet nurse and drove her off the estate, but her guilt could never be proven. No one ever found out what happened that night ... The mystery of it inspired me to paint Pampelune's second portrait.'

'Oh, really? Which one?'

'I can't imagine you haven't spotted it. It's massive! It would leap out at you! You are in dire need of spectacles, miss.'

Upstairs, the father, lying on the floor, trembles under the impact of the story being printed in his flesh that he is powerless to stop. Every sentence hurts him and reawakens the pain in his back. He hasn't grasped the earth-shaking power of the truth being revealed in veiled language through him.

Sleeping peacefully in the guestroom, the harridan ignores his complaints. She lives here now, and this bedroom is hers. She takes her afternoon naps in the comfy goose-down duvet and the sculpted pine bed after having written enough to dislocate her shoulder. She will no longer rearrange the pillow behind the father's back. Or pour the potent medicine over a sugar cube, counting the drops. Or wash him with a washcloth, empty his chamber pot, make a poultice, collect leeches in the pond, offer him a eucalyptus jujube, put fresh water in his glass.

Outside, the Dalmatian continues its carnage, devouring the poor little rabbits that imprudently tumble in the ferns. Red splotches join the black, which could attract coyotes and wolves. They used to devour plenty of sheep and birds, and even a little girl abandoned in the forest.

The old man heads down another corridor. Passing in front of a charcoal sketch, he offers a disinterested 'Oh, yes, I remember this one.' His enthusiasm fluctuates when he looks at his work – some pieces leave him indifferent, while others make his eyes brighten and well up. Leaning on his cane, Poedras goes into the large, abandoned living room. Old sheets are draped over the armchairs. If he were to run his finger along the moulding around the window, scrolls of dust would snow down. In the bookcase, the pages of books have yellowed, then browned. The wood of the sideboard long ago soaked up all the wax that had been applied to it. The housekeeper no longer ventures this far, and the furniture is thirsty. Poedras sniffs the air, like a dog. He spins around twice, laboriously, leaning on his cane, and declares himself dizzy.

A few steps take them down a bit lower, to another wing of Malmaison. The manor is a labyrinth. Aliénor supports the old man and helps him move around. They advance down a hallway where imposing portraits of all the fathers line the walls, some signed by the father of Poedras and some by his father before him, all sort of the same man as well. There is more than a century of history. To review the Berthoumieux genealogy, Aliénor points to the portraits, and Poedras identifies the subjects.

'The Buffalo Father, the Era of the Horn. The Passenger Pigeon Father, in the Era of the Wings. The Sheep Father, in the Era of the Sheep, and on it goes like this up to the idiot with the donkeys, in the Era of the Hoof.'

'And what about their wives? Why aren't they in the portraits?'

'To represent the estate, you paint the lords of the manor, those who passed on their name and their blood, who owned and fertilized the land by raising their livestock … History speaks nothing of the matrons.'

'But the women left so many traces in the forest!'

'You can admire their portraits engraved in the trunks of some trees. They left many other marks. You need to keep looking, my child. Your rage blinds you; your beautiful eyes haven't learned how to see. You need to open your heart wide! This forest hides another. Like Russian nesting dolls, the goddess harbours another woman. There is a doll in the doll, in the doll, a painting in the painting. *The egg is in the nest, the nest is in the hole, the hole is in the knot, the knot is in the branch, the branch is in the tree, the tree is in leaf, the tree is in leaf!*'

The artist does a little jig, but Aliénor doesn't feel like laughing anymore. The rage has filled her little partridge heart. She inhales, but the exhale doesn't come easily; the air is compressed and stays in her lungs. She turns blue.

'Oh! Your anger is so intense that you are burning from the inside! Take my hand and relax, or you won't last long.'

This old man, with his golden skin, his weathered face, his long white hair, and his magnetic aura, is the most beautiful man her eyes have ever gazed lovingly upon. She would take the risk of hiding in the arms of such a man, breaking into a thousand little pieces.

'I think I love you,' she whispers. 'Yes, I love you.'

'Speak up! With all the hair growing in my ears, I'm practically deaf,' he says, plucking a particularly long one. 'What did you say?'

'Nothing. I didn't say anything. Come on! Let's keep looking for the second portrait of Pampelune.'

Their exploring leads them to the small storage room where sacks of grain for the mill are kept, along with wooden crates to ripen fruit and jute bags filled with vegetables and roots that grow in the Centre: beets, rutabagas, pattypan squash, Jerusalem artichoke, ginger. On the wall shelf in the cold room, there is also a box full of glass jars, a few empty milk jugs, two or three grey wooden boxes, a large wicker basket … From this era, oxidized rings remain on the floor from pear and apple juice, its traces of ethylene lingering in the air.

The young woman and the old man walk past the laundry room, where three bags of starch are piled. There is also a large wringing tub and a washboard leaning against the wall. They approach the last room, at the back. A cradle and a roll of twine have been forgotten here, a long time ago. The cradle makes a sad creak when gently rocked.

A voice comes from the other end of the hallway. 'You won't find what you're looking for here.' The two visitors jump. Backlit, the silhouette of a woman is traced in the light.

Advancing toward them, the harridan is also reviewing the genealogical history of the Berthoumieux clan by circulating among the paternal portraits.

'First, the Buffalo Father, Era of the Horn, too busy milking, hoeing, reaping, too exhausted to desire anyone at all.'

'The story of the desideratas begins in the time of the passenger pigeon, under the reign of wings with the Goose Mother and her lady blacksmith. They were driven from the estate, then the village, run off like vipers. In a rustic house in Finistax, at the home of two women in love living on the edge of a cliff, there is a beggar's bench where a soothsayer spent the night. In reading their fortune in the entrails of a goose, he foretold a fate intertwined with desire and solitude and saw that they would go to their death hand in hand, letting themselves be swallowed up by the open void of the cliff. And that is what happened.

'In the Era of the Sheep, the Sheep Father wrote the next chapter of the Berthoumieux history; that's where the second line begins. He fell in love with Héléna, the speechless servant, who drowned in the fountain where her effigy was erected in marble. She draped herself in a veil and posed for the sculptor on the sturdy table where the lady blacksmith used to store her tools, always under the eye of the Sheep Father, who was jealous of the bond between artist and model. In the Perfume House where lived concubines, muses, and mistresses – the desideratas – a child was born of a forced union between the sheep breeder and Héléna. As soon as she was born, the infant was left in the cover of the forest, then taken in by a good man, a gentle giant: the trapper. Throughout her early childhood, he took care of her, fed her game, dressed her in fur, had her drink from the stream, and gave her a name. Her blue Berthoumieux eyes left no doubt as to her paternity. Around the age of five, she was sent to the convent orphanage.

'My name is Victoire, and I am that child who was dressed in furs. I am the daughter of the Sheep Father and the goddess of the fountain. I was never cold, or hungry, or hurt, and now I stand here before you.'

The artist and the young woman remain frozen for a moment in silence.

The housekeeper turned writer takes up the thread of her story. Because she never wants to let it go again. This thread of wool has to be pinched firmly between her fingers and woven into all the other chapters, one for each desiderata, one for each heir: she must weave the words, leave no strand of wool forgotten. And, deep in the night, wake up with this thread wound around her dreams, a slip knot that strangles thought.

'Shortly after my birth, Héléna, my mother, took her own life. The desideratas were not free to love the ones they desired. The pain was acute, and my mute mother did not have the words to tell her story. That eats away at you from the inside. It consumes you. It ends up winning out over reason.'

Through a window with open shutters, the water of the fountain can be heard flowing nearby. The swan-necked goddess listens to her daughter's voice. The seams are straining; the vanishing points converge; the three women have finally been reunited. Something – a shape? a story? an idea? – appears. A lineage is revealed.

The victorious harridan smiles at Aliénor and continues her story, because the story must be kept on a leash like a dog; one must not get distracted. The painter's white hair shines, as if electrified, hair that smells of herbs and tea and that makes Aliénor's heart beat.

'Chapter Three, the Era of the Hoof. They say that the Donkey Father, my half-brother, wanted to give Pampelune a stud farm and open a small-game hunting business; in other words, he had plans to launch the Era of the Horse. He could picture himself, sitting high on a fine steed with a golden coat against the backdrop of fall, blowing his horn to announce the start of a hunt after the fox has been released. The idea seemed sublime. But the father failed; his desire to look good and make his mark drove him to raise Akhal-Tekes, a breed too fragile for the Noirax climate. He managed to keep only mules and donkeys, not even good enough to be hitched, which he acquired to amuse children at fairs. This father interrupted the line of prolific breeders and became the show-off we now know.

'They say Pampelune was overcome with melancholy; she was too young and in love to be a matron in her own right and to erase herself from the story. Too sensitive and filled with desire to accept the presence of concubines in the other house. She challenged the order of things and wanted to be the father's only lover. She moved into the Perfume House herself to prevent other women from living there, as well as to extend her territory, particularly because of what she had seen and heard in the forest.

'Because while he didn't know how to breed them, he liked to watch horses run, so the father started betting on the races. Occasionally at first, without Pampelune knowing, then more and more often, until he was going every night. Placing sizeable bets, always on the wrong horse, he squandered part of the Berthoumieux fortune on galloping purebreds. To forget his bad luck and take his mind off it all, he threw himself into the arms and between the legs of one woman and then another. In a nocturnal cancan of bare thighs and hearts, he had more and more objects of his desire, growing dizzy as if on a ride. 'Unlucky in gambling, lucky in love,' he would say. I was one of them. I gave birth almost at the same time as Pampelune. After the two children were born, I was hired to take care of the little boy and the houses. I was just out of the orphan's convent; I was poor as a church mouse. I had no choice but to entrust my baby to the trapper who raised me in the forest, so that he could protect her and keep her somewhere safe until it was time to go to the convent, where she would be taken care of ... To correct the injustice, he gave this child the name of an empress.

Un nom de fleur en flames
Un nom qui charme et blesse
Un nom qui contienne assez d'or pour n'en jamais manquer
Un nom pour déclarer la perte et réclamer son dû
Un nom pour s'imposer et faire trembler les faibles
Un nom pour déclasser les pères et les soumettre
Aliénor

A name of flowers aflame
A name that charms and wounds
A name that contains enough gold to never run out
A name to declare the loss and claim what is due
A name to dominate and make the weak tremble
A name to relegate and subjugate the fathers
Aliénor

'To learn the truth, Aliénor, my daughter, you have to enter Malmaison another way. Learn to look behind the facade, through the pigment, dig through the heart of the home. You think you're in the house, but you haven't even set foot there yet. Don't tell me you came all this way to settle for standing on the threshold.'

hese revelations start a fire in her breast and turn on a light in her head. Aliénor runs, runs like white water and, like Pampelune in the forest, slips and recovers, knocks down the portrait of the Sheep Father as she heads back down the hallway, stumbles, and rips her pretty dress. Quick, quick! Back to the main wing. There is no more time to lose.

She grabs the blacksmith's twisted poker that is leaning against the hearth and, with its pointed end, slashes the hulking painting of Malmaison. She presses with the sharpened tip, and part of the canvas gives way. New details, in the windows of other rooms, have appeared on the painting in the meantime. In the guest room, a woman with purple and white hair is writing furiously by candle-light. And, in one of the three top dormers, a man is praying to make it stop.

There is nothing to do but to destroy the painting. In her haste, Aliénor severs the woven threads of the canvas. The secret has lasted long enough. There is a painting behind the painting! That is where the treasure is hidden! The hem of a dress appears. Pampelune was waiting for her in the heart of Malmaison. Standing in the grass, her narrow foot is revealed. A large swath of the first painting gives way, Aliénor cuts herself with the poker; a bit of blood spreads on the fibres of the canvas. It doesn't matter, she is in a hurry; the mystery has gone on long enough.

The hidden painting is revealed in an explosion of tender, luminous colours, jade green, canary yellow, pale pink, golden white, powder blue, splattered by dazzling, opaque light.

Wearing her wedding dress, Pampelune is standing in a pretty clearing of tender clover, a baby sleeping in a carriage on one side of her and a bouquet of pimparelas on the other. She is holding a slightly opened, transparent chest the size of a jewellery box, decorated with a lock embossed with a B. A ray of light illuminates the young mother's face, and the brightness prevents us from seeing what is in the box. The expression on the woman's face leaves no doubt: she is overwhelmed by panic and fear. She will have to kill or be killed. Not stay quiet, not assume she is safe, never forget her maiden name. Like a hunted animal, learn to detect the smell of death lurking. Disobey. *Pampelune Discovering the Truth* was hidden behind *Disobedience*.

Every time she gets close to it, the truth slips through her fingers like water in a fountain. Her nerves give out; Aliénor dissolves into tears.

'I don't understand all these riddles! What's in the box, under the light?'

'You're going too fast, Aliénor,' Victoire says. 'You're getting ahead of me. Let me write the story. Don't forget that your rage is mine too.'

'I'm tired of the twisting stories and shadowy chapters. I want to see what's in the blind spot!'

'All right, if you insist, I will show you. You want it, asked for it. So, hear the gunshot and the panicked run of a woman. The story begins with a bang.'

She goes barefoot into the forest. All that can be heard is her breath and her steps. This is not Snow White; no, this is Bluebeard's new wife. The trap is set, the hunt begins, the prey panics. Baroque music, beating drum, and a heart pounding the tempo of a metronome gone mad.

Suddenly, an echo can be heard, diffuse, from the other side of the pond.

A second gunshot. A feather drifts down in the dark night, a duck plummets, a dog barks and sniffs at the smell of gunpowder, fear. The void moon is a tiny crescent, a filament of light, the reflection of which drowns in the water while she tries to catch her breath and anxiety assaults her chest, leaving her no chance, like in a nightmare. She has to find a hiding place and fast, but the only place to hide is the burial cave, the Berthoumieuxs' charnel house. The massive door gives way easily under her hand, and Pampelune descends into the fathers' tomb.

A long staircase leads to the secret chamber. The *still desire of the effigies draws her in* and inflames her. In the Berthoumieuxs' tomb, she advances toward the dark heart of the cave. Pampelune stretches out in an unoccupied box bed and starts to sing, with her small, barley-sugar voice, as she does every night to get her son to sleep, until she can sing no more, her voice breaks, the fire goes out.

Étonnée, à peine née.   *Astonished. Scarcely born.*

Above her, someone closes the door and lowers the bolt. A man's footprints mark the earth along with other, narrower tracks.

Pampelune, dead among the fathers. Voilà. It is so easy to disappear.

There are still blind spots in the story, dark rooms along the hallways, songs with the last verse dropped that are starting to be forgotten and that people refuse to learn.

La chanson que tu chantes
Je ne veux pas la savoir
Je ne veux pas la savoir, sur le bord de l'île
Je ne veux pas la savoir, sur le bord de l'eau
Sur le bord du ruisseau

The song you sing
I don't want to know it
I don't want to know it, at the island's edge
I don't want to hear it, at the water's edge
At the stream's edge

Alongside the main family tree, a second story is unfolding and seeking the light: the story of the desideratas and their descendants, heirs with blue eyes, greenish skin, and purple hair. Yes, there were other sheds, bedrooms locked with a key, lost keys, old buildings sealed. The dead rest in sinister caves, and little girls in the belly of the wolf. The forest, a silent entity, is not the accomplice one thinks, except maybe for the coypus who continue to devour the young shoots of the horn tree. There will never be an end to this rabble.

The official family tree hides a forest of children left to their fate.

In the main living room of Malmaison, on the cherry bookshelf, there is a line of beautiful forest books about the art of bleaching deer antlers, hanging meat, preparing the heart of a bear. There is the illustrated dictionary of fox hunting with hounds; a book entitled *Spinning Wool on a Spinning Wheel*; the eighteen volumes of correspondence between a nun and a coureur des bois; old copies of the *Farmer's Almanac*; romance novels, airport novels, and noir novels; a little lower, at the height of a child's hand, *Songs, Tales, and Nursery Rhymes*, *The Most Beautiful Refrains*, and *La Bonne Chanson*; lower down still, a guide to edible mushrooms; an encyclopedia of native ferns; and, finally, way up high, with the spine facing the back, tossed behind the row of books devoted to the history and the geography of the central region, there is a notebook of Berthoumieux recipes written out by hand: creamy buffalo milk cheese, holiday stuffed goose, pigeon pie, boar's head cheese, lamb shank, glazed head, mustard-braised rabbit, grilled boar, butter with scallions, chives, and onions. The notebook also contains instructions to prepare green milk and other deadly decoctions infused with oleander and leaves torn from rhubarb plants. From the rhubarb they draw oxalic acid, or sorrel salt, generally used to brighten wood greyed by rain and the summer sun. Generally. If necessary, it has other uses. It takes only a few hours for the herbs to take effect. *The beauty will go to gather them*. It was a notebook meant for the matrons, a weapon stored in plain sight, on a tedious evening falling into the wrong hands – the hands of the Donkey Father. Your deadly tea is ready, dear wife. No, you will no longer go to the trees, Pampelune. The oleander has been cut. The father went to pick it.

You will no longer go anywhere, and you will dance no more. You know too much. You saw the little hand, heard the infants crying in the forest. You understood, and you wanted to end the systematic abuse and erasure. You naively believed you could do it on your own, that you could just move into the Perfume House to drive out the desideratas and their little girls dispatched into the woods. How gullible! You thought your will could trump that of the fathers; that is where you went wrong. Now you are trapped, lying in the cellar, numbed from green milk.

Fill the time, wait until dawn and give the herbs time to take effect. Time is heavy and filled with anxiety. The father's mind clouds over like the sky of Noirax before a downpour. Nothing more can be seen in all this greyish mauve. The father places the duck's still warm body in the cooler reserved for birds that have not been plucked. Yes, that's it, he needs to do small concrete things to keep his mind occupied for now. There are probably hares caught in traps. Weeds to pull along the wall. The father places the bird at the back of the small fridge. Oh! the pretty little cyan feather under the duck's sepia wing!

'Strange time to go hunting.'

He jumps. The housekeeper is there.

'You're early!' he says, surprised.

'I always wax the wood floors before dawn; it doesn't make any noise, and they dry before anyone walks on them.'

'I couldn't sleep so I went outside.'

'I have an herb that calms insomnia between seasons. I can make you an infusion.'

'No, thank you. I'll be fine. I think I'll go to bed. I'm exhausted.'

'Yes, I would imagine. Hunting is tiring. Good night, Bernard.'

Strange that she would call him by his first name. Strange and unseemly. He had planned to go back to the cellar but, because of her, the next step in the plan will have to be postponed several hours. He does not like to be hampered in this way by a will other than his own. The harridan is a bother; she is always underfoot.

'The house is sparkling ... Take tomorrow off.'

⁓

The sky of Noirax is pale, bled of colour. Lifeless. Like the practically moonless night and Pampelune's inert hand. The father lets himself be swallowed up by the forest. A boar passes, then another on its tail. There is the rustling of ferns that lean on one another in a slow caress and of a linden tree that lazily sways its branches in the voluminous September air. The piglets gallop in alarm to a crescendo, then their pace slows to silence.

It is as if nothing has happened, as if everything is as it should be, as if nothing has changed.

The father slides the stem of the bolt – a slight creaking joins the whisper of the trees and the wind. A quick descent into the round chamber, where a bed is made up for eternal sleep. He uses his hands as blinkers to avoid seeing the fathers who are sleeping down to their bones. There is not enough air. It is suffocating in the bowels of the cellar.

There is not a shadow of a woman here. Pampelune is not in her recessed bed, nor in the bed of any of the fathers. The chalky smell of blackened hearts permeates the space and muddles perception. He lowered the bolt … He is sure of it! There is no way Pampelune could have escaped! The father feels duped, forced to go back over his plan. He definitely saw her: Pampelune was wearing her wedding dress and lapping up the green milk. She drank the whole cup, then, overcome with spasms and hallucinations, wanted to return to her perfumes. The father saw her run at top speed through the forest, arms reaching out before her, paranoid, escaping into the dark night, singing that her candle was out and that a fire had to be lit, the heat of which would be delightful.

The desire to kill her still stabs at his gut.

Stunned, contrite, he goes back to Malmaison, talking to himself. He has looked at the matter from every angle. Conclusion: someone is toying with him, trying to humiliate him, or else he is losing his mind.

The pale dawn sets in, at first like a maiden's blush, then baby pink from the palette of roses.

As he requested, the housekeeper is conspicuously absent. The father gulps down a quail's egg and an apricot, hesitates between a coffee and an Armagnac, opts for a glass of mineral water, then goes up to bed.

A woman is lying in the marriage bed.

The foul smell of dead, wet, rotting flowers.

Lying on her back under the wool blanket, head swallowed by the downy pillow, no sound or movement. The father advances on tiptoe, recognizes the golden lock hiding the face. It is like Sleeping Beauty, after she was pricked by the spindle of the spinning wheel. The father's hand starts to gently tremble, like water coming to a boil in the kettle. Abruptly, he pulls back the blanket, and he sees her.

Pampelune, in her wedding dress, sleeping for eternity, her cheeks blue and her eyelids closed, sewn shut, with the open mouth of the dead that can swallow the night.

econd shot, the dull sound of a duck dropping, then a beagle barking.

From the window, I saw her, panicked, trapped, head into the woods, then enter the cellar to die among the fathers. To mark the time of the beginning of the hunt, I stopped the hands on the grandfather clock.

I followed her into the forest, wearing the husband's shoes, to leave his tracks. I, too, went down into the charnel house. I saw the other fathers sleeping like kings and Pampelune, poisoned, in a box bed. I bundled her up to hoist her onto a jenny's back. I brought her back to where she belonged, the marriage bed.

The next day, they pointed fingers at me; they drove me off the estate. They hissed at me as if I were a witch; they threw stones at me. And the years passed. Cycles of the moon and seasons, the births of many foals, many snowy winters, and a few village mayors. Now I'm back.

It's easy to disappear, a lot more complicated to reappear.

In the forest, an old, defoliated tree falls in indifference.

❧

Aliénor opens the transparent box where the father stores the pile of missives. First surprise, they are not letters, but official documents. Nervous, the young woman rummages and sifts through them. The box that was hanging around all this time on the table, in plain view of everyone, contains dozens and dozens of birth certificates – including her own.

The result of the Donkey Father's incestuous union with his half-sister Victoire is Aliénor, half-sister to Jeantylle, the blue flame flickering deep in her left eye.

❧

In his bedroom, the father screams and writhes in pain, but no one comes to his aid. The story is tearing at his body more than ever. Outside, the painter's Dalmatian continues the carnage, sinking its maw into the bellies of hares and smearing red all over the canvas.

'The air is heavy here; let's sing,' the old man suggests.

He does so in a quavering voice.

La laine des moutons	*The wool of the sheep*
C'est nous qui la tondaine	*We're the ones who shear it*
La laine des moutons	*The wool of the sheep*
C'est nous qui la tondons	*We're the ones who shear it*

Let's shear, let's shear the wool of the sheep, sings Aliénor's blood mother, Jeanty and Jeantylle's milk mother. Two families, two lines: one that pierces the light and shines in the day, the other that makes its way through the dark and the night.

The anger has calmed in Aliénor's breast. Despite the shock of the discoveries, she is breathing more freely. She can relax her jaw now that she has found what she came to find in Noirax. What is left to do but sing? She sings along with the painter and the writer. *Let's shear, let's shear the wool of the sheep.*

❦

Away from the Berthoumieux estate, far from Noirax and the wool to spin, Jeantylle goes to the big city, where metamorphosis is possible. She is wearing Aliénor's kaleidoscope dress, the one the harridan made with the seams showing. It's the first time Jeantylle has gone out like this in the world, and she is a bit nervous.

Walking along the Boulevard Grand-Axe, the young woman studies her reflection in the window of a large store. From certain angles, Jeanty still exists. Disappointed, she lifts her bust a little so the androgyny gives way to femininity. Heads turn as she walks by. Jeantylle puffs out her torso to make her chest stick out. A businessman smiles at her and whispers what sounds like 'pretty little filly.' Jeantylle blushes, tucks a lock of hair behind her ear and arches her back.

When she sits at a terrace, a waitress appears.

'What is your desire?'

'I will have an allongé and a warm croissant, please.'

'Your wish is my command, Miss.'

The sun kisses her cheek as the aroma of roasted coffee rises in the big city air and blends with other intoxicating smells that carry on them chapters yet to be written. Existence is increasingly heady. In her pocket she pats the key to her new apartment.

❦

The converging lines have finally come together into a point.

The three women have recognized each other.

The halves have been reassembled.

Two sexes exist in the mirror for a single heart.

They have penetrated the house for good, destroyed the evil, exposed the secret.

The milk, the blood, and the pink of their solution.

The fractures coexist.

The wool is spinning and allows itself to be braided.

Prepare your brushes, artist Poedras. To soften the bitterness of the reunions, we are going to paint a lovely new portrait, outside, beside the goddess. A chickadee will settle on her messy chignon. This family portrait will replace the one that has just been destroyed. How beautiful it will be, all these people gathered together, bonds woven, tied tight! How merry it will be, a family finally restored.

But the links are still entangled; we have to continue to sing, to write, to rebuild, to undo the knots. To unravel the sheep's wool.

VI

WE WON'T GO INTO THE
WOODS ANYMORE

very morning, Victoire writes furiously – furiously indeed – to make up for lost time. When writing this way, a strange flame lights up her eyes. It's a desire that makes the pupil shine, something insatiable, but somewhat assuaged in the doing, and the excitement – carnal, consuming – gives birth to the act of creation.

Writing is crying wolf one time too many and being alone with the animal, believing that we have domesticated it, but ultimately being devoured.

The road to her den is filled with obstacles; it is difficult to get to. You need to tack, not look behind you, and, once there, go as deep as you can, let yourself be sucked into the vortex to probe the infinite possibilities. It's not so bad if you don't come back and the wolf eats you.

The woman writing in the shed wakes at sunrise with words already in her head, mad, fresh, spinning ideas and, when she falls asleep at midnight, she can't wait for the next day to get back on the merry-go-round, and so on, until the curtain falls on the final page, until the six letters of the words 'the end' take their place beside each other, the ideas settle back down, and calm is restored, however fleeting. The desire to write about all sorts of subjects – about the little girl who was offered a dog that was too big, for example – comes back, unstoppable, and she has to give in. Obviously, the dog was a wolf, but we don't know for the moment whether it will devour the little girl. It would be nice if sometimes the little girl prevailed.

To describe the tender hue of pink of some people's flesh, Victoire does not use the expression 'maiden's blush.' The language no longer belongs to dirty old men. She writes 'flesh pink,' simply, and leaves the reader the choice of the object of desire. We could also not mention the colour, since the French word for the flower – rose – contains the colour in its name. What comes first, the flower or the colour? We could also compare the pink of roses to the pink of the gums of canines. Every word is a labyrinth, a descent and an ascent, the end of all possibilities. The sentence is like a treasure hunt; the treasure is the story that is built like a house, an old manor, a storybook village, a strong perfume, a memory.

Animals naturally approach the woman dizzy from writing. She attracts salamanders, frogs, cicadas, grasshoppers, and old painters who want to talk.

'When I was a young man, at the beginning of my practice, depicting reality became an obsession. Hence the number of still lifes that hang on the walls of Malmaison. How I loved painting the perfection of a fig stem, the detail of the veins of a spinach leaf, the glint from a window on the smooth skin of a pomegranate, the centred fold of a tablecloth and its lace edge. The russet plumage of a pheasant. A floured country loaf. The glistening seed of a pear … But reality is impenetrable. Words and strokes of colour merely skim it. With each work, we stumble; it's a losing battle. Don't you find that tragic?'

'The battle isn't lost; there is everything to seize and to gain. I write to cheat death,' Victoire exclaims, before blood starts to stream from her nostrils to her lips.

She pinches the bridge of her nose until a clot forms. Then she gets up and says: 'The world appears in all its richness only when I write. Writing is the key that unlocks the doors to memory.'

She swallows some blood and sits back down.

Do they know that they are characters in a play, made of paper, ink, and pixels? That their destiny weighs heavily, but that they have no shadow? That Noirax is trapped in a novel, that they are living a still life? That the story is starting to fall apart? That once they head away from the estate and the houses, the structures fold down like the lifted squares of an origami fortune teller forgotten in the pocket of a little jean jacket to be found the following spring? Room is being made in the wings, because the end is near. Soon they will have to store the set.

'I am one hundred and three years old and I am tired. It is no longer up to me to carry the history of Noirax. I am putting the torch in your hands; this is the real reason for my visit to the estate. It is also a burden to keep alive the memory of beings, things, and land. Victoire, you are a storyteller, raconteur, chronicler, witness, biographer, dramaturg: a writer. Without words, the village would not exist, the forest would stop breathing, the manors would crumble, the perfume and memories they contain would fade. You substitute yourself for *He who observes us from on high, as if from the seats of an ancient theatre.* You will decide on the direction the hares take and the intensity of the lighting. Writing is more than describing; we are not shackled to reality.

When Victoire asks him to go on, he cloaks himself in mystery and lets it be understood that it is now up to her to provide the answers. The more she insists, the more he digresses.

'Words are hollow, bubbles of air! Be careful, Victoire, that they don't burst in your face!'

'Words are electric! They are the life than runs along the paper, to make the little marionettes move and dance.'

'This forest is a dream, and you will invent the words to cross it!'

Before yielding to fiction, Victoire became a biographer out of duty to memory, to set down on paper Aliénor's childhood, in every way similar to her own. The mother and daughter meld into one orphan queen. Victoire told the story of the first few years in the forest, sleeping on a bed of moss, curled up in fur, until she went into the convent, where they taught her to keep house to earn a pittance and live the life of the poor. At age sixteen, her hair shorn and disguised as a stable boy, Aliénor ran away from the convent, getting hired on livestock and agricultural farms. She learned to *plant cabbage the local way*, in other words *with elbow grease, the local, local way*. Like the jennies, the mint, and the horn tree, Aliénor could survive anywhere, rooted in any kind of earth. Pretending to go home after work, she would go to sleep in the granary, in the reassuring fragrance of wood freshly chipped.

Victoire curbs the desire to invent details, to alter events so the story seems even more true, predestined. Her natural inclination takes her further from experience, makes her want to imagine, to touch what is true by way of what is not. The call of fiction is as seductive as the siren's song, as exciting as the wolf's impending arrival. But first she has to establish the facts, let the truth be known. Writing kills secrecy and settles collective memory. Yes, she has to cry wolf!

After Aliénor's childhood, there was Pampelune's death to tell. Victoire wrote it like a police statement, trying to fill the hidden chapters with little bursts of poems, snippets of songs, and even melodies.

Some stories demand to be sung. Others to be played, after being modelled on the three unities of time, place, and action. But classical theatre is rigid; the flexibility of the novel is better suited to lively minds like Victoire's. Exploding under the pen, tales and fabliaux emerge, short dark stories set in dank manors inhabited by diaphanous women on the edge of a forest that may be home to a wolf.

'He isn't there, so he won't eat us.'

Yes, Mr. Poedras, we all heard your billy goat's voice.

Once Poedras has left the estate, Victoire will return to the shed to invent a new story that features an old painter.

And then, a caustic little tale featuring wolves on a beach that attack a group of young people having a picnic, eating grilled meat and drinking rosé. An altercation erupts between the people and the animals. Threats, shots, cries and growls, bites, blows, flesh ripped open, fur torn. During the attack, the humans and the canines each lose one of their own. As a prelude to the story, there will be a puppet theatre, with excerpts from 'Little Red Riding Hood' or 'Peter and the Wolf.' At one point, the children will laugh loud, very loud; they will be in high spirits, as if infected by their own laughter. But, after three little turns, their smiles will disappear, and they will set off running, screaming in terror that the wolves have arrived. Then the hands will emerge from the cottony interiors of the puppets, and we will return to nature and to the lives of pack wolves in the forest. Yet another story hiding a second.

Poedras is eager to paint them both, Victoire and the gleam in her eye, wide open to take it all in, Aliénor and the bright pigments of her expelled anger. He leaves, hobbling with Médor at his side, while, all around him, half-devoured, dismembered, disjointed, the hares die.

With the snap of fingers, we have left the theatre to enter the depiction of a small-game hunting scene with, in the distance, an old painter, his cane, and his hunting dog.

The painting is entitled *Scarlet Still End of Life*. It was painted with delicate brushes made of the fur of hares, on a hemp canvas coated in primer, then pressed on a wood panel. The year of its creation is not yet recorded.

winter has passed since the painter's last visit. The snow has had time to fall and then melt, and the mushrooms to mushroom again. Summer is radiant, in full bloom. The sky of Noirax is tensed under the threat of a summer storm. While waiting for the heat to fall with the rain, the animals take refuge in cool groves. On the forest road, holding the quivering body of a partridge, Aliénor emerges on the set.

In the writing shed, the tender thorns of the blackthorn are slowly macerating in barrels to make the eau de vie they will drink in the fall when they need to warm their throats. They will submerge plums and cherries in the Troussepinette and use the sediment to infuse the fruit.

Offerings were left at the feet of the marble goddess. Roses and frangipani flowers, sections of orange, tangerine peels, sticks of incense. A few coins and accompanying pious wishes have been tossed into the fountain that Héléna eternally fills with her tipped jug. This morning, camellia flowers have opened completely, unfolding all their petals, revealing a heart of golden pistils. The chlorophyll is at its peak, and the forest appears denser. Sounds of wings beating in the foliage of a tree; on a branch, a woodcock swallows a caterpillar in abrupt jerks. Much lower down, between the roots of an elm, a young wolf scratches at the ground with its paws, then eagerly digs. Beyond the neighbouring vineyard, in the treetops of the evergreens, young vultures stretch their wings for the pleasure of the glide. At the base of the old trunks, small, round mushrooms, soft as velvet buttons, flourish. The estate is a horn of plenty. You just have to reach out your hand to grab a piece of fruit, an animal, a cep, a spray of thyme and make the most sumptuous of meals.

The Berthoumieux fortune has imploded. On the advice of the notary, it was divided and transferred by force. 'Get on your knees, Bernard. Beg pardon, otherwise you will rot in jail, eat pudding with a lead spoon, and sleep among fools in dirty underwear, in a burlap sack, on a flea-infested pallet.'

Now, the father Berthoumieux pays rent to live in Malmaison.

A crowd of heirs is still prowling around the manors. They are preparing to go back to their lands after claiming their fair share. The father's assets have been redistributed among all his descendants. Coming from Saud, the Hauts-Pays, Ouestan, Finistax, and even the archipelago of the Mer Basse, they have the blue irises of the Berthoumieux family, the red, brown, purple hair, depending on the desiderata who gave birth to them and sent them into the forest. They are the ones who placed on the white marble pedestal, at the foot of the goddess Héléna, their forebear, wishes, prayers, citrus, myrrh, and resin. This line produced only girls, who, like Aliénor, are now relieved of their rage. The truth both weighs heavily and lightens the load. Its fragrance is the same as newborn babies, sweet milk, curds and cream, the smell of vernix caseosa.

It is the moustachioed good doctor who is elected mayor of Noirax, and Bernard Berthoumieux is doing much better since he is no longer under his care. Forced to withdraw from the opioids, he went through a rough time. His fantastic wounds, from which magically emerged small objects of no value – baby teeth, shells, streamers – have completely closed up. Using Jeantylle's magnifying mirrors, the father examines his back. There are no more grooves or scars, no physical trace of his misadventure. It is as if he hallucinated the whole thing. Since coming off the drugs, the encounter with his heirs and the dispossession, he sees life in sepia. It happened suddenly: one morning he opened his eyes and life had turned brown. He doesn't tell anyone about it, because it's not the first strange idea he has had, and, when one cries wolf too often, eventually no one believes it, and the wolf finally shows up. The father has gone half-mad. Sometimes he lounges in his housecoat on the balcony, looking out over the estate. The sweet air of the Centre fills his lungs, enters his room, and makes his curtains billow – just like before. He closes his eyes to stop the monochrome of purplish browns, to see life in colour again, and it's as if nothing has changed, as if he still enjoys all his privileges, minus the desire to dominate and the domination of desire.

In the father's dreams, a desiderata dances on a horizon that is out of reach, further and further away, eternal ballerina in a jewellery box, turning while tinny mechanical music plays.

The villagers have resumed keeping little gardens, where they gather over a glass of eau de vie. Noirax breathes easier. Joy returns, quivering gently at first, like sap in the trunks in spring.

Under the aegis of the new mayor, the region's economy catches up with the times. They produce sulfite-free wines, they grow soy and peas, the chickens lay their eggs free-range, and pesticides, force-feeding geese, and strawberries the size of your fist are prohibited. They plant cabbage the contemporary way. They have even discovered a promising mineral deposit. The soldiers have returned from their postings. A new generation of children will soon jump for joy in the streets of Noirax.

Activated by three of the Sheep Father's heirs, the rotor of the Jorle Mill happily turns and mills, breaking hulls, grinding rye.

✧

From the top of the stairs, the father looks down at the acacia table. On the cracked kaolin plate, Aliénor lays *apples, pears, pineapple, soda, soda, soda crackers*. A few nuts, coarse peanuts, and a jackfruit – the fruit of the poor, how embarrassing! – listless on a porcelain plate, appealing to no one, certainly not her. The country loaf is defrosting in a single-use plastic bag beside a jar of grape jelly. There is tempeh and soy milk. Pea soup. A can of sardines and sliced eel in oil. A block of tofu. The guts and offal of a non-dominant boar float in a blackish liquid that looks like bile. A retch rises in the father's throat. The table was a lot better when the housekeeper was not a writer. To finish the table, the body of a partridge set down on the tablecloth is discordant with the rest.

'Please prepare it as confit; we will eat it tonight with a warm salad with pears,' Aliénor commands. 'The pears poached.'

The father smiles. He likes to obey her, even since learning that she carries within her the red of his blood and the blue of his iris.

Aliénor, his daughter, the one who stripped him of privilege. And here she is grumbling like a child.

'This local wine will be the perfect pairing, so stop wincing when you look at the bottle.'

The father hates the floral taste of orange wines. They make him nauseated; he far prefers the frank character of assertive varieties, Syrah, Grenache, Merlot, which never have an effervescent finish, like a little insult imprinted on the tastebuds.

Sitting in the middle of the food that is uneven in its appeal and the wine that already displeases him, there is a letter from Jeantylle.

Aliénor makes herself sardines on bread and settles in to read about her half-sister's adventures. Jeantylle documents her arrival in the city, her first steps on the asphalt, with or without high heels, depending on her mood that day. It is a lot of change in a short time, but she has never been so convinced of her choices. Jeantylle bought herself a couture dress that the father will assess with the same enthusiasm as orange wine. She likes to cross the city with its lights to come home at the wolf hour and live a life leagues from the melancholic days she spent in Noirax. In the city, she can give free rein to all her eccentricities, bloom like a tree rooted in good soil, with adequate light, watering, and fertilizer. Boar hunting, wielding bows and arrows, gathering wild garlic, the constant braying of the jennies, feeding the hearth, the dampness of the stones, the paternal portraits, the ghost of Pampelune, her boy's underthings, and her rugby ball: all of these burdens that kept her on the ground, prevented her from taking flight, she has left far behind. The young woman no longer wants to live in a still life painting. Where the forest holds its tongue, complicit in all the buried secrets, the city, full frontal, headily reveals and exposes itself … You have to bite into the fruit, eyes looking straight on. Run as fast as you can, even in stilettos, at the risk of cutting corners, because the set will soon collapse!

At Aliénor's and Victoire's invitation, Poedras set up his easel in front of the Perfume House. He came without his dog because, since the carnage among the hares, Médor is no longer welcome on the estate. Despite his trembling hand and blurred vision, the painter will capture the second manor for all eternity. Armed with his brushes and the omnipotence of the artist, he will decide on the direction of the ivy's deviation. Maybe for once he will let it rise toward the light? He has never tried. It might be amusing to tangle with reality and stick to it entirely, now that no one expects it of him.

The horn tree has stopped growing in the garden. The roots have all been chewed up by the coypus. The still incomplete absinthe fountain has remained trapped in bubble wrap. Aliénor has boiled no spirit, there will be no green fairy at the estate, only Troussepinette like everywhere else. After the donkeys, no new animal era will keep the Berthoumieux land busy, but new human lives will emerge from the bedrooms of the Desiderata House. The smell of death will be chased out by the intoxicating scent of babies; Aliénor is overseeing construction so that divine children can be born here. *Let us rejoice in their birth.*

From the new mayor, she obtained authorization to give the second manor a new vocation; it will be transformed into a birthing home. Not much is left of the cracked furniture, other old things, and mould that thrived here. Walls were knocked down. Before being rebuilt on its foundations, the house was purged of its contents, then exposed to the open skies, uncovered to chase out all the expired perfume and dark ideas. The interior was rethought, redesigned, then divided into bedrooms for the women giving birth. Life will flutter and bloom here.

The foreman can't get over all the old chandeliers, all the relics accumulated. The Berthoumieuxs lived in another era, according to other mores, like in ancient times. He likes it when the little lady with the smouldering eyes gives him orders. It unnerves him, pleasantly unsettles him. He likes responding to her demands and making her happy. He is always probing her with his eyes, hunting her with his gaze; he would like to align his north on hers. One day soon, he will place his huge hand on the little lady's stomach, and between her thighs. She will share with him her treasure and all the ideas of grandeur that inhabit her. He will warm her when she is cold, care for her when she is sick. In the meantime, driven mad by her stray black locks, her two different-coloured eyes, and her rough manners, he is subject to Aliénor's charm.

When the new house opens its doors to mothers-to-be, the young cep merchant will be retrained as a midwife. With her velvety voice, she will hum her favourite song into the ears of newborns while Odette and Rita knit them little mitts in soft wool.

The renderer will clean up the blood from the births and dispose of the placentas.

Victoire will record in her great book all the births, those that will be added to the branches of the many genealogical forests of Noirax, which she is working to completely restore. No heir will be forgotten; they will always be welcome on the estate.

The father will put his nose to the grindstone as well, will dirty his hands, because he will be charged with feeding the women well, an art at which he has always excelled. He will prepare meals both nourishing and delectable to help the new mothers recover. The father will cook new plant proteins cultivated in Noirax with, for seasoning, the nearby forest, a cornucopia where flavours abound. Every day he will have to inquire as to what the new mothers want and grant them their wishes.

Many new babies will continue to be born in Noirax. Even if the set falls and the story is interrupted before next spring, a final melody will be played on the oboe, with the accordion resonating, to accompany the cries of the latest infant of the story. As an echo to the music and the cries, we will then hear the braying of a jenny, the anguished cry of a buzzard, the supple step of a starving wolf that arrives.

When, between chapters, Victoire lifts her head to think about what comes next in the story and of all the possible endings, her chair creaks. In the paper forest, she pushes aside the branches of the genealogical tree to see the birds painted by the old painter whose hand trembles in the liquid colours.

When fictional life has stopped here, there will remain the still lifes by Poedras.

The grapefruit and the half-peeled lemons on the table to represent the bitter fall.

The hourglasses, the drooping flowers, and Pampelune's skull with candles set in her eye sockets will symbolize time passing.

Decks of cards, dice, jewellery, fans, coats of arms, pocket mirrors: here is all the vanity of the world assembled.

And finally, feathers and fur bound together, hare, goose, pheasant, and a bouquet of herbs, to recount the joy of one who feeds with delight.

We have crossed the forest.
Now the curtain may fall.
The wolves are among us.

TRANSLATOR'S NOTE

Sing, Nightingale features many traditional children's song lyrics, which have been translated from the original French. The lyrics appear in both languages except where they are run into a paragraph.

The original French novel, *La désidérata*, features archaic and obscure French terms that have been adapted to modern English in the translation.

The novel also incorporates references to works by Quebec authors and songwriters, including Michel Tremblay, Élise Turcotte, Anne Hébert, and Gilles Vigneault. Often these are referenced by title; these allusions are often lost because the works in question haven't been translated into English or have been translated with a different title.

SONGS AND WORKS CITED

'À la claire fontaine,' French traditional, pp. 13, 28, 34, 48.

'Cantique des étoiles,' French traditional, pp. 32–33.

'La p'tite hirondelle,' French traditional, p. 36.

'Le petit roi,' Jean-Pierre Ferland (1970). Courtesy of Editorial Avenue and Editions Renlec. p. 47.

'En passant par Lorraine,' French traditional, pp. 55, 59.

'Nous n'irons plus au bois,' French traditional, pp. 62–63, 146.

'L'arbre est dans ses feuilles,' written by Zachary Richard (1978). Published by Éditions du Marais Bouleur, administered by Third Side Music. pp. 69, 136.

'L'Empereur, sa femme et le petit prince,' French traditional, p. 79.

'Malbrough s'en-va-t-en-guerre,' French traditional, pp. 82–84, 88.

'Alouette,' French Canadian traditional, p. 85.

'Ailleurs,' Corbeau (1982), Marjo (1990). Lyrics by Marjolène Morin. Courtesy of Thésis Musique. pp. 89–90.

Légende de la Pimparela (the legend of Pimparela): From a legend that appeared in *Histoire Du Doyenne: Et de la Paroisse De Moyrax du XI au XX Siècle* (1908). Inspired by Jean-Pierre Campesan during a picnic in Astaffort in March 2014 (tour for the Prix France-Québec). pp. 92–97.

'Meunier, tu dors,' French traditional, p. 94.

'Bon roi Dagobert,' French traditional, pp. 98.

'Dansons la capucine,' French traditional, pp. 103–4.

'Au clair de la lune,' French traditional, p. 108.

'Ne pleure pas, Jeanette,' French traditional, pp. 109–11.

'The Tomb of Kings,' from *The Tomb of Kings*, Anne Hébert, tr. Peter Miller, Toronto: Contact Press, 1967. pp. 116–17, 144.

'Les litanies du feu,' Quebec campfire song, pp. 117–18.

'Ah! vous dirai-je, maman,' French traditional, pp. 120–21.

'Promenons-nous dans les bois,' French traditional, pp. 125, 159.

'V'la l'bonvent v'la l'joli vent,' Canadian traditional, pp. 126, 173.

'Vous dirai-je, maman,' French traditional, p. 134.

'Isabeau s'y promène,' French traditional, p. 145.

'La laine des moutons,' French traditional, p. 151.

'Savez-vous planter les choux,' French traditional, p. 158.

'Les pommes,' French children's rhyme, p. 164.

'Il est né le divin enfant,' traditional Christmas carol, p. 166.

Marie Hélène Poitras was born in Ottawa and lives in Montréal. She received the Prix Anne-Hébert for her first novel, *Soudain le Minotaure* (2002, reissued by Alto in 2022; *Suddenly the Minotaur*, DC Books, 2006). Her short story collection *La mort de Mignonne et autres histoires* (Alto, 2017) was a finalist for the Prix des libraires du Québec. While *Griffintown* (Prix France-Québec and finalist for the Prix Ringuet) was inspired by her experience as a carriage driver in Old Montréal, *Sing, Nightingale*, an ode to creation, draws on her travels in the French countryside.

Rhonda Mullins is a Montreal-based translator who has translated many books from French into English, including Jocelyne Saucier's *And Miles To Go Before I Sleep*, Grégoire Courtois' *The Laws of the Skies*, Dominique Fortier's *Paper Houses*, and Anaïs Barbeau-Lavalette's *Suzanne*. She is a seven-time finalist for the Governor General's Literary Award for Translation, winning the award in 2015 for her translation of Jocelyne Saucier's *Twenty-One Cardinals*. Novels she has translated were contenders for CBC Canada Reads in 2015 and 2019 and one was a finalist for the 2018 Best Translated Book Award. Mullins was the inaugural literary translator in residence at Concordia University in 2018. She is a mentor to emerging translators in the Banff International Literary Translation Program.

Typeset in Trade Gothic Next Pro, Adobe Jenson Pro, and Camelot Caps.

Printed at the Coach House on bpNichol Lane in Toronto, Ontario, on Zephyr Antique Laid paper, which was manufactured, acid-free, in Saint-Jérôme, Quebec, from second-growth forests. This book was printed with vegetable-based ink on a 1973 Heidelberg KORD offset litho press. Its pages were folded on a Baumfolder, gathered by hand, bound on a Sulby Auto-Minabinda, and trimmed on a Polar single-knife cutter.

Coach House is on the traditional territory of many nations, including the Mississaugas of the Credit, the Anishnabeg, the Chippewa, the Haudenosaunee, and the Wendat peoples, and is now home to many diverse First Nations, Inuit, and Métis peoples. We acknowledge that Toronto is covered by Treaty 13 with the Mississaugas of the Credit. We are grateful to live and work on this land.

Edited by Alana Wilcox
Cover design by Ingrid Paulson
Interior design by Crystal Sikma
Author photo by Charles-Olivier Michaud
Translator photo by Owen Egan

Coach House Books
80 bpNichol Lane
Toronto ON M5S 3J4
Canada

416 979 2217
800 367 6360

mail@chbooks.com
www.chbooks.com